Something To Remember You By

Something To Remember You By

(original title: September Song)

Vicky Martin

SCHOLASTIC BOOK SERVICES
New York Toronto London Auckland Sydney Tokyo

ISBN: 0-590-09950-7

Copyright © 1969, 1971 by Vicky Martin. This edition is published by Scholastic Book Services, a division of Scholastic Magazines, Inc. by arrangement with Thomas Nelson, Inc.

14 13 12 11 10 9 8   0 1 2 3/8
Printed in the U.S.A.

CHAPTER ONE

APRIL SAT AT the kitchen table with her chin resting in her hands. She thought for a moment how well it fitted there, slotting in perfectly to the hollow of her palms, and then she lifted her head and looked out over the bay. It was at its very best, navy blue and quiet, with the sun having a glorious last fling, splashing the occasional boats that carved little furrows in the sea. The gulls rocked complacently or did aerobatics. Everything was unchanged. Everything to be registered and loved. She smiled and then dropped her chin back into its resting place.

They had arrived that afternoon, overflowing from the car and tired of the journey, and the house was waiting for them, crouching securely among the patchy grass with the sea looking over its shoulder. April had unlocked the drive gates, falling towards them in her eagerness and then standing aside to let the car pass. She had breathed in so deeply that she was almost dizzy. Down the short drive, stretching her hands to touch the green delicacy of the tamarisk bushes and then running round the bend and seeing the house again. A year in between — that was nothing. She had watched her family, struggling a little in the sudden freedom like newly born things, and the spaniel running in a frenzy, and then she had gone down to the beach gate and just looked. The beach was empty. The August lot had spread themselves in fortnightly heaps and gone pink and packed and left. September was for the inmates, for those who knew and loved the coast enough to brave it when the chances of sun were small and the chances of the big Atlantic wind great. April had stood by the gate with the long month spread out ahead in her imagination like the sea, refusing to think of anything beyond September. A *whole* month this time, just because of alterations at school. A month. She would use it and love it and when it was over she would be able to face the looming horror of exams and plans and a future. Her hands, needing to move, had locked themselves against the bars of the gate and she had thrown her weight back and dipped her head until her body arched away from the gate and the sea. That was how she had felt that afternoon. Steel-strong and curved. This summer was going to be the best ever.

The few hours between the beach gate and now had been patchily filled with unpacking and unlocking and eating. They had eaten early and the twins were sleepy and angry, spooning in tomato soup more erratically than usual. Still a little withdrawn from the journey and the sudden lifting of them all from one place to another, April had been quiet, watching her family and not being with them. Sandwiches left from the picnic and Bess, her mother, mopping and calming the twins; a brown banana that nobody wanted in the middle of the table. Her father, deep in one of his withdrawn moods, making acid comments and eating hugely. Davy considered that any holiday gave him a dispensation from the diets he plunged into sporadically throughout the year. Milk, warm from the car, and digestive biscuits that had crumbled at the edges and Pan, pink-faced and silent, her spoon moving rhythmically from bowl to mouth. And the spaniel, begging and being pushed away, begging again and succeeding. The vague, untidy meal trailed away when Bess gathered the twins and took them to bed.

April had experimented with an idea for the last couple of months — the idea of dividing into separate incidents the things that happened in a day. Journey, arrival and the jig-saw of unpacking, the meal. The twins — she had gone upstairs with Bess and watched her mother, who was streamlined by years of experience, as she undressed and washed and supervised teeth in one smooth process. The twins had given way to obliging quietness, curled in their beds like small animals with their identical faces peering over the rim of sheet as though they were looking out

3

of envelopes. Mima, with old Bear in one hand, had been asleep before Bess knelt to kiss the small bit of face which escaped between sheet and hair. Honey sat up suddenly, her face stricken. "I haven't got Quilty!"

"Oh Lord!" Bess turned to April, pulling a disaster face. They searched through half-empty cases and drawers for the ragged square of rather smelly blue towelling that Honey couldn't sleep without. Every now and then Bess stole it away and washed it but Honey always knew. "It doesn't smell right!" April had found Quilty in the toy bag and Honey clutched it thankfully and leant up, putting a starfish hand each side of April's face and kissing her. Honey loved kissing. In the passage, closing the door quietly, Bess had whispered, "Thanks."

Another segment, back in the kitchen, Bess taking a cigarette from her bag and lighting it thankfully. "They're asleep."

Slow talk between her parents that April wanted to join with but didn't know how. Talk about nothing and yet it was important.

"When are the others coming?"

"Tomorrow afternoon." Bess looked in vain for an ashtray and then used a plate. "Susie rang me yesterday. She'll come down with the boys and stay two days. Then she goes back and she and Peter leave for Spain."

"How long will the boys be here for, then?"

"Most of September, I think. I suggested that Susie and Peter come down and pick them up and stay a week if they want to."

4

"Going to be a bit crowded, isn't it?" Davy bent his face down.

Bess ground out her cigarette. "Not in the least. Susie and Peter can have the spare room and the boys can go in the big attic. Paul's driving them down, by the way. He passed his test a couple of months ago."

Davy made a grumbling, lion noise. "Well, I hope he drives better than his mother!"

April, playing with a small heap of crumbs on the table, said, "What are the boys like now?"

"Of course, you weren't here at Easter, were you?" Bess smiled. "Mick is exactly the same, just as small and serious and clever and his glasses are even thicker. But Paul is completely adult. The twins adored him."

Jealousy had touched April then. It came whenever she thought of the spring, of all of them here without her. She had been sent to France for a month to improve her limping French and get a bit of experience of a world outside home and school. She had loathed it, learning French avidly in a desperate attempt to get something out of the awful month. Such a waste of a holiday. The open warmth of Paris, fighting to get her brain to think in strange sounds and shapes, and at night longing for the house and the wind and all of them. "I never want to go to France again," she had said, holding Bess for a moment at the station, and they laughed.

Bess had smoked two cigarettes and the talking lapsed and Davy stood up very carefully because the driving tended to bring on his lumbago. He gestured weakly towards the plates and Bess grinned and waved him away.

"Not tonight. I'm too tired."

"Mrs. Gill will moan," Pan said.

"Too bad. We'll stack." Bess gathered plates and cutlery like playing cards and heaped them on the draining board. She worked so fast that it was almost impossible to help her without slowing her down. Biscuits into tins, milk in the fridge, butter and bread sorted away, and then she took the remains of the picnic coffee and went out to join Davy. Pan hovered for a moment and went too.

That had been the last segment, April thought. Left alone, she had moved to the window seat and drawn patterns on the steamy window with her finger. This room and the sea were hers now. She loved both. The kitchen was the hub of any house Bess controlled and this one could have been designed specially for her. It was the place you came to first to tell anything, or if you were looking for someone, or if you were just bored. It gave food, music from the tinny little radio that Bess carried everywhere, drying places for wet clothes, and a hospital section for damaged children and animals. "No, not rats!" Bess had said last year when Honey came in with a limp grey body. "I won't nurse rats!" Honey, five then, had crumpled and screamed at the discrimination.

This room, big and square and facing the sea, gave a ship feeling. Not many chairs because of the long window seat. A dresser, running all down one wall, that received them the first day with its blue and white china in neat rows and dissolved, after a few hours of occupation, into chaos. It was permanently heaped with pots of marmalade and dog biscuits, towels and plastic mugs and bowls of cooling jelly. Green jelly. The curtains were never drawn and at night the bay was spread out like a black quilt. It was a good place to dream in, the kitchen at night.

But not now. Not this particular night, April thought. Jerking herself out of the slow contemplation of the last few hours that always helped her to accept the change of scene, she moved. She felt restlessness growing and she wanted to take it outside onto the beach and let it grow against rocks and sky and she wanted company. As if by telepathy, Pan came in, drifting aimlessly. April reached towards her very cautiously.

"Coming onto the beach, Pandy?"

Pandora looked up, surprised by the words and the tone. The three-year gap that separated her from April had grown enormous in the last year. She studied April with narrow blue eyes. She shrugged: "OK."

They went sedately outside and then April broke into a run and Pan, after hesitating for a second, followed suit. They streaked across the grass and from the wooden seat Bess watched them go with a smile. She wanted her two elder daughters to be friends as she and Susie were friends. The twins had each other and would need nothing else, but April and Pan . . . three years was a difficult gap to bridge. Bess longed for her children to be uncomplicated. Their odd moods of independence or rage or sudden affection frightened her, although they came and went so abruptly. She had bred temperamental children.

April unlocked the beach gate and led the way over the rocks. She knew every crack and surface and she went fast, her bare feet making no sound as she jumped from rock to rock. She stopped on a high ledge and sat, cross-legged, waiting for Pan to come up and join her. Pan was sedate in her movements, as though her puppy fat somehow robbed her of bounce. She sat carefully beside April on the ledge. She was painfully aware, and had been for the last year, of the contrast in the way they looked and she was wary of April now, unsure of her sister's moods and motives. The invitation had delighted her but she would have died rather than show it. It didn't do to show weakness to April. She would notice it so openly that the person who displayed it would be damaged.

"Isn't it beautiful?" April hugged her knees.

"I suppose so." Pan wondered at the obviousness of what April said. Of course it was beautiful. She knew that, as she knew that April was beautiful. Aunts whispered it and girls looked enviously at it and boys had begun to see it now. The only person utterly unsure of her beauty was April. Pan studied her sister secretly, seeing the stillness of April's body. She always seemed coiled, ready to spring suddenly and frighten you. She put up a hand and touched the straight red-brown hair and, unconsciously, Pan touched her own cropped, curly head.

"Do you think it will be the same, Pandy, ten years from now? We must come here and remember all of this and this evening."

"We won't remember now in ten years. Now isn't that important."

"It is and we must. We'll bring our husbands and children here."

"Husbands?" Pan circled the alien word warily. She disliked the entire male sex in a dispassionate way, apart from her father who didn't count. Boys, men, different in a way that disturbed and enraged and demanded competition.

"You might not be married, of course. You won't be quite twenty-three."

"Mummy married at twenty-two."

"I know, but lots of people marry later." It frightened April to set a time limit. To not marry, to live alone forever, was as terrifying as the idea of death. If she set a limit at twenty-two, at twenty-one she would start worrying. In five years she would be twenty-one and she hadn't even started with men yet. Marriage and love and sex, from the outside, were so incredible. April imagined that a huge change would take place and make her different and able to understand. She dropped her head a little and her voice was self-conscious. "Most of the girls at school have boyfriends. They write to them and talk about them a lot and things."

Pan sensed that April wanted her to say something but she didn't know what or how. She groped, wanting to reassure April and at the same time wanting to rest for a moment in this new, totally unsuspected power. "They probably talk about them more than they really are."

"Mmm." April moved her hands up to her knees. "Do you think I'm pretty?"

"Of course. You're going to be beautiful. Everyone says so."

"Do they?" She caught hold of the reassurance. She wanted to say, *When? When?* Then she had a burst of humility. "I wasn't much good at that party last week. I stood round for ages and Jane's mother was there. Can you imagine, having the mother there? She introduced me to this creep who was smaller than me, much smaller, and he didn't speak. Awful — we just stood not looking at each other and then he said, 'Would-yer-like-ter-dance?' and grabbed me. Instead of dancing properly he was doing ballroom stuff. He trod over me and everyone was looking." She giggled. "Jane was with her man with her arms round his neck and someone turned out all the lights and everyone started kissing, except some girls who were by themselves. Pandy, he breathed all over me." She half laughed but the agony was clear in her memory. Not to be chosen by one of the tall, older men. To be with the creep, pushed on him by Jane's mother. At sixteen, April had been one of the older girls there and she was still utterly out of her element. All her friends seeing and knowing, and she had watched them using the tricks and instincts that they must have

10

been born with and she, tragically, had not. To have no sex appeal was terrible. Perhaps she was frigid too. The thought of the creep's mouth made her shiver horribly.

"They were probably all too young," Pan said, and she knew as she said it it had been the right thing to say. The only thing. She rushed on, "You know how it is in books and films, it's the older men who appreciate . . . well, they probably kissed whoever they were with, that lot. Whatever it was like."

April turned and smiled brilliantly at her sister, curving her mouth up into a radiant thing and tilting her eyes into paisley shapes and Pan felt the full glory of being April's confidant.

The moment passed. April said, awkwardly, "You'll be pretty when you're older, Pan."

"No, I won't. I'm fat."

"You'll get thin and you'll be the right height, not too tall like me and . . ." She groped, realizing now that she should have prepared her facts before she started. "Your hair is a super colour."

"It's orange."

"It's super. We'll be the two beautiful Miss Roberts, pursued by fantastic men and driven in E-types by pop stars. . . ." She grinned and Pan returned the grin a little uncertainly. She didn't have as much opportunity or inclination for dreams as April did.

They sat for a little until the coldness of the sea wind and the recognition of the end of the interval made them go back. April relocked the

11

beach gate and they made their way into the house.

The kitchen was empty. "D'you want cocoa?" April said.

"No, I'm going to bed." Pan had had enough contact for one evening. She had nearly always put herself to bed, even as a small child, knowing instinctively that she needed a lot of sleep and peace. "Good night." She closed the door.

April put the milk on to boil and stood over it, stirring in the cocoa and sugar and watching the milk get busy round the edges of the saucepan. She felt intellectual and mystical. She forced her eyes to stare into the fawnness of the cocoa and tried to force her mind into the future, but she saw only the illustrations of her thoughts. When the milk boiled she gave up and poured the frothy cocoa into a mug. She took a cigarette from the half-empty packet her mother had left on the table and sat on the window seat, drawing smoke inexpertly into her throat. She was unsure of her family's reactions to her smoking. It was the whole performance that appealed rather than the taste, but the thought of appearing self-conscious was ghastly. Bess smoked wildly, waving her cigarette as she talked and scattering ash, brushing it off her clothes and leaving soft grey marks. April wished they could see her smoking tonight. She was doing it so easily. She looked out of the window. It was quite dark now with a shy moon dodging in and out of streaky bacon clouds. Long after the cigarette and cocoa were finished she sat very still and she felt wonderfully old.

The house was very quiet when she went up to her room and her room was waiting for her, curled in its familiarity. That afternoon, dragging her suitcase down the passage and finishing with a spurt that carried her through the open door and down the two shallow steps into her bedroom, she had been struck, as always, by the whiteness of it. The sharp white light of the sea. She had slept in this room for as long as she could remember and, like the house, it never changed. Bess had said, a couple of years ago, "Shall we paint your room, April?" and had been angry at April's ungracious "No!" Bess had shrugged big shoulders; it had been just an impulse, easily pushed aside. She wasn't interested in decorating and only when a room became blatantly slummy did she feel stirrings of guilt. But she had been hurt at April's reactions. April hadn't tried to explain. It was obvious, surely, why the room must stay the same. It was her room, a corner room, looking out over two different aspects of the bay. A low door in the outer wall led onto a balcony and steps corkscrewed down to the garden. Low ceiling, lino worn thin, finger marks on the paint as familiar as her own face and the patterns of the dried-out damp stains on the ceiling. She loved the room as it was and fought passionately against invaders.

"Would you like to have Pan sleeping with you? We could get another bed in." Bess had tried that tactic in the phase when April and Pan were three thousand years apart, not three.

13

"No! Please!" Two years ago, "no" had been April's most frequent word.

Tonight the room enclosed her. She drew the curtains, shutting out the night view, and unpacked some more, piling clothes into drawers. A great heap of old jeans, shirts and canvas shoes and the new bikini. She laid it reverently by itself in a top drawer. Last year she had worn and loathed the school bathing suit, embarrassed because it was tight across the bosom. She had been very late getting a bosom and Bess had forgotten and stared blankly when April hinted about a new bathing suit. But this year the bikini. As with smoking, she was unsure of their reaction and slight nervousness came to her when she pictured herself in it. She shut the drawer.

Her mind wandered and her hands slowed until the unpacking stopped and she folded, cross-legged, on the bed. So much of her was tied up in this room. Incidents flashed at her. Last year, unpacking, she had stopped and looked at herself in the scarred long mirror, moving thin hands down her body, wondering, her head on one side. Giggling from the doorway made her swing round and it was Mima, peering through, her face full of delight at having caught April.

"Get out, you horrible little watcher!"

"Why?" Mima stood on the top·step, her skinny body stiff with obstinacy. Taunting.

"Because this is my room."

Mima's tongue came out, slowly and luxuriously, and then as April sprang at her she leapt

14

back, laughing a half-delighted, half-frightened laugh. April chased her down the stairs and outside and Mima ran to Bess and that had started the first day off with tears and shouting. Mima turned on tears effortlessly and Bess took the wrong side, her face changed to a series of angles and planes by the tolerant smile that enraged April so much.

She shut the memory away. This year she was crossing the line into the adult camp. No more competing. Last year had been bad. Fifteen — a young fifteen she knew, which didn't help — and she had been too old to play with the twins, ashamed of splashing and shouting and fishing the shallow pools with them, although part of her still loved it. This year she was sixteen which was an age, not a gap to be lived through. She had talked a little to Bess in the spring on one or two funny evenings when they had found themselves in the same place and in the same mood. April lay back on the bed and smiled. She wouldn't be embarrassed by her father now. She pictured his heavy-stomached figure in the old blue bathing trunks, his big laugh, the way he looked running into the sea after the tiny white bodies of the twins. These thoughts carried affection, not awkwardness. She wouldn't blush anymore at his sudden, unanswerable attacks of sarcasm. The wonderful oldness came to her again — a feeling of infinite achievement. She had reached backwards, to Pan, and been accepted. Forwards, too, to her parents, and almost accepted there. She thought of the third way, the way she hadn't reached yet, and it made her close her body together, head on knees, arms wrapped round, and anticipation quickened through her. She thought of reaching towards men.

CHAPTER TWO

BESS WOKE AT seven, her supersensitive ears detecting noise from the twins' room. The sacredness of early morning was one of Davy's basic laws. On no account was any noise to be made until the twins had an official visit from a parent, declaring the day open. Bess glanced across at her husband. He was sleeping heavily, his large body cocooned in quilt, and she slipped quietly out of bed. The last thing she wanted was to start the holiday off with a row so, the permanent trouble-dissolver, she crept across the passage. As she opened the door she heard scuffles and found the room very still with two motionless figures curled in the wreckage of their beds.

"I know you're awake," Bess hissed angrily. "You mustn't make a noise and wake Daddy."

"But it's day." Honey opened her eyes.

17

"You know you can't get up until I come and tell you." Her voice was slow and dangerously patient. "Look at your books." Her stark morning face was stern, hiding the sympathy she felt. She could remember the agony of wasting the early morning, of staying in while the world happened outside. She relented, holding out her long, soft arms and they came scrabbling to her, pressing their bodies against hers and tilting up small, penitent faces — faces she hadn't been able to tell apart till Mima grew more hair. Bess kept that difference between them now so that they would have separate identities. Mima's hair hung halfway down her back. Honey's hair ended abruptly where the small white neck began and her eyes looked out from beneath a thick fringe. Bess smiled at them. They were irresistible in this mood. She marvelled again that they were only there because of her carelessness. They should never have been conceived. She untangled herself and tiptoed out, finger on her lips, whispering, "Only half an hour." How stupid. If you are six, half an hour is forever.

She was completely awake now so she went down to the kitchen. The spaniel welcomed her and she let it out, watching it go mad across the lawn. It was rather a misfit. When it first arrived, all feet and eyes, they had thought of fantastic names and discarded each one as unworthy and then it was too late. It had become "the spaniel" or "it." Pan adored it and it treated her with vague contempt, ignoring all her efforts to train it. She had spent hours, armed with soft biscuits, pushing its bottom down onto the grass and saying "Sit!" The spaniel swallowed the reward and allowed its bottom to be pushed down until all the biscuits were gone. Then it would streak off. It owed allegiance only to Bess, probably because she fed it.

Bess made some tea and restrained the impulse for a cigarette. She always wanted one when she woke, regardless of the time, and although she might not smoke again till lunch it seemed so debauched to smoke early in the morning. An insult to the new day. She drank her tea on the window seat, cotton nightgown curving round her thick body, and she pondered food plans and the day ahead. A complicated mingling of personalities would evolve. Brightly coloured people, dazzling and bruising and warming each other. By the time Bess had finished her second cup it was getting on for seven-thirty and she poured one for Davy and carried it up.

Her husband, too, was appealing in the morning, Bess thought. He came out of sleep like a train from a tunnel, blinking at the light, his thin hair ruffled to look thicker. "Tea." Bess waved the cup slowly backwards and forwards and the steam curled up in loops. Davy grunted and attempted a smile and groped for the cup, lifting his face for the kiss Bess shed. He steadied the cup as Bess got back in. Through his daze came slight irritation and he gradually realised the cause. Susie was coming.

Davy had never understood his wife's sister, still less reconciled himself to the fact that two

19

sisters could be so totally unalike. Bess was a mother. Vague and marvellous, she had abandoned all claims to being attractive when the twins were born. She dressed in what happened to be nearest to hand in the morning. She wore shoes only when she had to and she had beautiful feet, incongruous under her big body. In the summer they were burnt brown, the toes small and undistorted like a child's. Susie . . . Davy sighed. Susie was two years older than Bess and she had married in her early twenties and had never forgotten that in her youth she had been a bit of a *femme fatale*. Her pointed ears were pierced and she wore earrings that swung when she moved and Susie moved often. At forty-five, a good figure and a low, husky voice and a sharp, theatrical mind made Susie a woman to be reacted to — one way or the other. Davy pushed his dislike aside and tried to work up sympathy. Susie adored her two sons, pouring out onto them all the love and attention her husband didn't appear to need.

The before-breakfast space was quite useless to Bess without newspapers. She picked up the book April had recommended. "You must read it, Mummy." It was beautifully written and deep, April said. Bess demanded action from books and after ploughing dismally through a couple of pages of superbly drawn characters and subtle dialogue she put the book away and went for the twins. They followed her into the bedroom, launching themselves from the door like small flying bombs. Davy was feeling fatherly and tolerant now and he lay, very much the lion, watching the antics of his brood.

April woke late and felt the guilty jerk of missing things that was left over from childhood. She subdued it, registering the coolness of the pillow and the light through the curtains, and then she stretched her body until she thought she would break. The curtains were moving a little as the wind played with them. She got out of bed slowly, experiencing pleasure because the dressing gown she put on was white and Victorian and ruffly, the lino cool under her feet, and she went out onto the balcony, swaying a little so that the ruffled hem of her dressing gown made small, crisp noises. It was going to be hot. The sun was already slightly hazy, a warm thing against her face.

Singing from the kitchen came trickling up the stairs and grew louder as April got nearer. The familiar reedy voice, well into the third verse of "Daisy, Daisy, give me yer answer do . . ." Wide back at the sink trembling as the voice came from it and reddish elbows and arms and hands were busy in the soapy water. April went quietly up behind the figure and put her arms around it.

"Merciful God!" The woman at the sink swung round, soapy water running off her hands, and she clutched April to her flowered overall. "I might have known it would be you. The little ones aren't so silly!" Her voice was high-pitched, permanently surprised, warm. "You've changed.

We missed you at Easter, I can tell you. Didn't seem the same." Her thin face went on moving after the words were finished.

"I missed you too, Mrs. Gill." April stood away from the large body. "How's your husband?"

"No worse, that's something." Mrs. Gill turned back to the sink. "I've got to get on. Yer aunt's coming and there's beds and veg to do."

April smiled and reached for the cereal packet and poured herself a glass of milk. She perched on the edge of the table, feet swinging a little. She loved Violet Gill as she loved the house and now she watched Violet's familiarity and it made her smile. Violet had worked for her grandmother but at sixty she was as energetic as she had been at twenty. Her huge, long body would tackle anything and she cared for her invalid husband devotedly, secretly glad of someone to look after now that her children were grown.

"Read anything good lately?" April and Violet Gill always discussed books.

"One novel. Romantic and a bit farfetched. Well, I thought that and then I thought about Nell Gwynne. Look at her. Nobody could have started off with less and then the King's eye fell on her and her life was nice, wasn't it? One of those rags to riches stories but worth reading."

April listened, crunching the corn flakes. Then, as an afterthought, "Where are they all?"

"Fiddling with the boats."

"I should think they need a bit of fiddling with after six months." She slipped off the table and handed Mrs. Gill the bowl and glass. "Bit more for you to wash."

Violet Gill's voice, in full spate again, followed April back up the stairs.

April found them gathered round the boathouse, the only occupants of the beach. "Hello," Bess said, "you slept late."

"I know." She peered into the dark interior of the boathouse. It was old, far older than the house, and the back was hollowed out of the cliff. The stone floor was uneven and great beams held the roof up. They had pulled the small sailing dinghy out onto the slipway and the two canoes still rested inside. April went in and looked at them. They lay close together like two lovers who weren't speaking and she touched their rough canvas. She liked the dampness of the old boathouse, the wooden platform along the back heaped with nets and sacking, oars and fishing rods. And the huge oak doors that had fought off storm after storm. April turned as Bess came in.

"I'm going into the village to stock up with food for the weekend," Bess said.

"Need any help?"

"It's all right. If you could just keep an eye on the twins. Davy's driving me in and I think Pan's coming."

April nodded, liking this woman-to-woman talk. "I'll try and get some crabs this afternoon. The tide should be right."

"Good idea." Her mother's voice had become

absent and April followed Bess's eyes to where the twins were kneeling over a rock pool. Without speaking she went out, crossing the slipway to them, her sandals slipping a little on the shingle of the beach. Mima held up a bucket proudly and April looked in and saw only seaweed.

"What's in there?"

"Seaweed and sea."

"Ready for what we catch," Honey explained. "Mim thought of it."

"Clever!" April borrowed a net and caught a small, unsuspecting shrimp which was dropped quickly into the prepared bucket. This filled the twins with new enthusiasm and they waded about the pool, making stabbing darts with their small nets.

April sat on a rock and watched them idly. The sun was stronger now and the sea very still, almost no wind. She lifted her head and sniffed, trying to smell a storm as the old fishermen did, but she smelt only the new-born decaying smell of the sea. She watched her father examining the canoes that he had pulled out, thick with concentration, and she watched her mother go to him and drag him reluctantly away, turning to wave as they went up the slope to the house.

"Where's Pan?"

"Drawing." Honey pronounced the word beautifully; the twins' delicious lisps and distortion of words were fading fast. Mima didn't talk about "wocks" anymore. It had been a silly question anyway, April thought. Pan was always drawing. She had a special little suitcase which she packed

24

with sheets of paper and pencils with dark, soft leads and lovely squashy rubbers. She used chalks and charcoal and she had been drawing for so long that the family accepted it and thought little about it. But Pan was good. Sometimes April would see one of the drawings and although she knew nothing about it, she sensed that they had something. When Pan drew cats they were catty and when she drew the twins, although there was no likeness, she caught the stiff-legged bounce of them. When she was younger, Pan used to take her drawings to Bess. April had been there one day when Pan came to Bess and held up a bit of paper. "Look, Mummy, I've drawn you."

Bess, busy with potatoes, glanced and smiled and said, "It's very good."

Pan had crossed the kitchen and crumpled the drawing into the wastepaper basket.

"What should she have said?" April had asked, unscrunching the drawing.

"She should have asked if she could have it." Pan grabbed at the paper and tore it up.

April went crabbing as soon as they finished lunch. She left the others spread in the sun. Bess allowed the twins to rest outside when it was hot, in the shade. "At least I can see they keep vaguely still!"

April crossed the slipway, a red plastic bucket in her hand. The tide was very low and after the first dry rocks she moved into a different land of smooth rocks, like eggs, garnished with seaweed. Brown and bright green seaweed, transparent and opaque, slippery and crackly, it trailed among the rock pools. She stopped sometimes and looked into them and then moved on, down towards the retreated sea. From years of experience she knew the best places to find the flat pink eater crabs. She wore shorts and a shirt, knotted up under the bosom, and old canvas shoes that gripped the slippery surfaces well. At the first good rock she stopped and bent down, flinging back the fringes of seaweed and peering into the cracks. A crab. She started to probe with the thin, strong metal hook. The crab backed into its sanctuary, its claws scraping against the rock and snapping at the tormenting hook. Suddenly, April got it, hooking behind it and jerking it out. It slithered scratchily onto the rock and she picked it up, one hand each side of the pink, matt shell, and dropped it into the bucket.

She moved on, from rock to rock, kneeling in front of hopeful places, getting some crabs and missing others. The little ones she freed, and they scuttled sideways into the seaweed. The sun was really hot now, beating down on her head and arms and finding her neck where the heavy hair divided and fell over each shoulder. She was completely absorbed, stopping only occasionally to straighten her back. The bucket filled, a moving mass of crabs.

She stopped for a rest after a couple of hours, sitting on a small dry rock. The tide had come up a long way and the best places were getting covered. April screwed up her eyes against the sun and looked back up the beach. Only a few figures were dotted across it. She watched one that was moving towards her, coming freely across the rocks as though used to them. As it came nearer she saw it was a man. She made out a striped T-shirt and dark hair and then suddenly recognised him and stood up, waving wildly. "Paul!"

The figure approached rapidly, growing as it came, and April began to wonder how she had recognised him. He bore little resemblance to the boy she had known last year.

"Hello, Paul. Look at the crabs." She held out the bucket. "Record catch."

He was beside her now. "Magnificent." He looked up from the bucket and smiled. "You've changed a bit."

"Not as much as you. You've grown up a little. Not quite so skinny as last year!"

There was laughter between them but not easy laughter. "Thanks!" Paul transformed his face into something very alive with his smile. "I knew I'd get a wild welcome."

"When did you get here?"

"About half an hour ago. They said you were down here." He paused and the slight shyness between them came further out into the open. "The tide will be too high soon, won't it?"

"Yes, the best places are covered already. Anyway, I've got enough." She climbed carefully off her rock and they started back up the beach with Paul carrying the bucket. He took it out of her hand, surprising her for a moment, and deep-

27

ening the shyness she felt. The seaweed, half dried by the sun, was like ice and April misjudged a bit and slipped and she felt Paul's arm almost lift her back onto her feet.

"Thanks." She laughed a little, surprised at his strength. Last year she would have teased him about it. Now, although the words came into her mouth, she didn't give them sound. She glanced at him as they travelled up the beach, the silence between them surprising her more and more. There was something about Paul that hadn't been there before and it disconcerted her and made her think of what she was going to say before she said it, and so she said nothing. She wondered if he felt the same. Then he turned his head and met her eyes and they smiled, seeming to slip back, almost, into their old friendship.

They reached the slipway and went up the slope to the house. On level ground, April realised how tall he was. "You really have got big, haven't you?"

"That's the second time in ten minutes you've remarked on my immensity."

"Well, I'm surprised, that's all." She laughed, half-closing her eyes against the sun. "How tall are you?"

"Six two. How tall are you?"

"Five nine." They stopped for a moment and looked at each other as if measuring. April looked up at Paul and liked the sensation. He looked down at her. Then they laughed, self-consciously, and started across the lawn towards the others.

An odd group of chairs, faded deck chairs and a couple of modern aluminum efforts and the old wooden seat, these things contained the family. The sounds were fast and lively. The twins, playing with their tea set on a rug, looked up when they heard Paul and ran to him. He gave them a hand each. Walking beside him, April felt Susie's scrutiny as she approached. Susie was holding court, reclining gracefully in a deck chair, cool in yellow linen. She held out a hand to April and gave a cheek to be kissed.

"But haven't you grown tall. . . ."

April smiled weakly. She suffered this comment from all her relations. What did they expect her to do? Remain a midget? It was like saying, "But haven't you grown old!" She sat on the grass beside her aunt, answering Susie's enquiries about school, Easter in France, plans, and as she talked, she became conscious of her untidy hair and old shoes. Susie always woke this reaction in her — an awareness of the way she looked. The familiar, earthy scent clung round Susie. April, folded on the grass beside her, wanted to wear scent herself.

Paul dragged the twins away from the bucket of crabs and carried it inside and there was an air of waiting about them all, April thought. For tea, probably. Davy was guiltily scanning his paper because he knew he should be attending to Susie. Pan, dragging blades of grass out of the earth and burying a small stone. Bess, catching up with the gossip with Susie. "Where's Mick?" April said.

"Mick's got a telescope." Mima made the word long and beautiful.

Susie laughed attractively and April suddenly saw the likeness between her and Paul. Their faces had the same way of becoming merry under laughter. The same dark hair and the way it grew back from the forehead and the ordinary features that blended together into something far more attractive than it should have been. It surprised April that she noticed this. Paul's face, which she had known all her life, had been as familiar to her as her own. Perhaps the year that had gone, through which they hadn't seen each other, made it necessary to look again. She wondered if Paul were doing the same to her. He was talking to Davy now and they were two men talking together. She felt a small jealousy that Paul had managed the transition so well. Paul, her cousin, almost a brother, had retreated and changed into something quite unexpected. She crossed her legs at the ankle, noticing that they were already beginning to go brown, and her eyes went back to Paul again.

Mick appeared, a small, jerky figure, glasses shining in the sun. "Hello." April smiled up at him, at his familiar awkwardness. "I hear you've got a telescope." As she said it, she knew it sounded the kind of thing an adult says to a child.

"Yup." Mick hovered and then crumpled onto the grass, sitting awkwardly, his shyness very obvious. He tried to hide it by looking precise and April felt herself wanting to smile at him. He was near her, near enough to talk to, and she couldn't think of anything to say to him. She tried, "What's the sudden interest in telescopes, Micky?" and he jolted into life and launched into an impassioned explanation.

"Can I help with the tea?" Susie said.

Bess shook her head. "Mrs. Gill's doing it all today. In your honour. She adores you, Sus!"

Susie laughed. "I won't fight!" She leant her head back, watching Bess get clumsily out of the deck chair and go towards the house. Big, smiling Bess, her hair tied back with a scarlet scarf that did nothing for her colouring and her feet bare. Susie loved Bess but she suffered pangs if they met in London for lunch or went to a wedding together. She smoothed the yellow linen down across her legs and arranged her hands. Her eyes swung down to April. It was lucky, she thought, that April's skin wasn't the dead white sort that burnt red, like Pan's. Or the sort that freckled all over, like Bess's. Susie stared and thought, *Why, the child is almost beautiful!*

CHAPTER THREE

HALF-PAST SIX till half-past seven was always the most frantic hour of the day for Bess. Twins to be bathed and put to bed, the evening meal and the spaniel to be fed. Tonight there was much more. Susie, Mick, and Paul to be arranged. Towels to be found and coat hangers that were always scarce in the house and Bess moved in quick circles. Tonight the twins were difficult, full of energy and angry, and they made each other worse in a kind of competition. Bess ran the bath and turned to find Mima missing. She went to the top of the stairs and screamed for her, pushing a strand of damp hair back from her forehead.

"I've got her." April appeared round the bend in the stairs with Mima. "And Mrs. Gill says she's done the crab and the potatoes are on and she's going now."

"Fine. Bring Mima to the bathroom, will you, love?"

Two of them, undressing wriggling bodies, watching for the wickedness to dissolve into tears and by the time the twins were bathed both Bess and April were damp and angry and the bathroom was chaotic with water and sponges and rubber ducks.

"Stay where you are and I'll get your supper." Bess was hot. She wiped damp hands on her cotton skirt. "April, can you bear to stay a bit longer and see they don't escape?"

"OK." In the end she stayed while they ate, reading an incredibly boring story about a rabbit. A kind of half-witted rabbit that got lost in a wood and, inevitably, found again. But the twins seemed to love it. They knew it by heart, shouting bits aloud. As she read, April could hear her mother in the room opposite and she knew that Bess would be attempting to look tidy for dinner. It was always the same, the effect that Susie had on Bess, as though Bess looked at herself in the mirror that was Susie and saw bare feet and faded cotton skirt and neglected hair. So, the first night, there was a big effort. Tomorrow, Bess would be back in warm untidiness. When the story had limped to its obvious ending April snapped the book shut. "Time's up." She took the trays out into the hall and went back, settling the twins and lighting the night-light. She had just got them tucked in when Paul put his head round the door and they sat up and bounced out of bed, ignoring April's shouts. She felt the annoyance spread across her face.

Paul gathered them up, one under each arm, and sat on Honey's bed. Their laughter was deafening. April stood watching, her hands moving uncertainly. She lacked the courage to let her anger show with this new Paul. Three figures on the small bed, laughing and moving, and just as April got ready to step forward, Paul tucked Honey deftly into bed. Then Mima. And they stayed there, giving in at once when he changed his face to seriousness. He winked at April. She turned away a little, wanting to hide the expression that she knew was on her face. Jealousy was showing again, that he could cope with them so effortlessly, so adultly. She bent and kissed the twins, elaborately affectionate.

In the passage, closing the door softly, Paul said, "I'm sorry if I disturbed them." He pushed his hair back from his forehead.

"It doesn't matter. You settled them again." Her irritation ran through her voice and she turned and went quickly down the stairs. He watched her hair swinging against her shoulders until she rounded the bend and disappeared.

They played bridge after dinner and the big, square room became small, diminished to the area of light round the green table and the four players. Cigarette smoke everywhere and in the silences the soft noises of the sea outside. April crouched in the big chair and watched them. The way the light touched them and made her father look irritable as it ran down the creases in his forehead and beside his mouth. It showed the raised veins on his big hands. It showed Bess's nervousness. She was partnering Davy and playing badly and annoying him. When her brain was called on to reckon odds and use rusty skills, Bess lost all confidence. Her hair was untidy again and the blue cardigan with silver threads became, on her, just another garment. Susie, immaculate in red, sat playing crisply and causing Bess's tension. By tomorrow, Bess would have gathered round her the security of her home and children and be content to herself again, but tonight she saw Susie, small and exquisite, dark hair sleek and hands red-nailed. Tonight Bess was the plainer younger sister again. She tried to compete in Susie's field and was damaged by her own failure.

April's eyes went, as they had so often in the last few hours, to Paul. She seemed incapable of doing anything but watching today. She saw the affectionate way he responded to his mother's attentions, to the small glances that Susie threw, and she thought she sensed a small thread of irritation running under Paul's smiles. She could only see his profile. It was more handsome than the front view of his face, older and sterner, and as she watched he turned sideways and smiled at her, a little uncertainly. Ashamed of her earlier jealousy, April smiled back and the smile was meant to say sorry and to promise future friendship. Susie, glancing up for no reason, caught the smile and stiffened slightly.

Now the restraint of the room, of herself arranged in the chair, began to tire April. She got up and went through the glass doors onto the veranda and out to the sea wall, swinging her legs over. There was a big moon and a deep, sea peace and these increased her restlessness. She tried to imagine what she looked like to the others if they looked out. More and more she was becoming conscious of herself and what people thought when they looked or listened. Tonight, changing into navy trousers and a white sweater for dinner, she had stopped by the mirror and shaken her hair forward and looked at her face. Between the heavy frames of hair, it was narrowed and interesting. She touched the reflected mouth and thought about Susie and brushed mascara onto her eyelashes. She had tied back her hair so that it fell in a thick, silky bunch. Now she pulled off the rubber band and let her hair fall over her shoulders. She looked up at the house. There was a light on in Pan's room and remembering the previous evening on the beach, she swung herself off the wall and went back in.

She went into Pan's room without knocking, without thinking, and she was stopped suddenly, amazed and almost shrinking from the face Pan turned to her.

"Go away!" Pan was facing her, ashamed of the evidence of tears.

April was thrown utterly off-balance, awkward at being embarrassed by Pan. "I'm sorry."

Pan came past her and pushed the door shut. "You could have knocked!"

"I didn't think about it. We never knock. . . ."

Pan was looking at the floor. "I didn't mean it. You just surprised me." A quick look into April's face and the tears were dismissed by both of them. There was a little, heavy silence. Pan wanted to talk but this situation — April, very still in the middle of the room and trying to cover her surprise — these things made it difficult to start. "Are they still playing?" she said weakly.

"Yes." April went to the bed and perched on the edge, her hands slowly sorting through the pile of drawings. She held up one of the house, a pencil drawing, hoping desperately that she had chosen the right one to comment on. "I like this."

A flicker of pleasure in Pan's face. "It's all right." She came and leant casually against the small chest of drawers, her hands linked in front of her. "Why do they have to come? Why can't it be just us here? Mick's awful." Her voice was low and cold. She looks ugly, April thought dispassionately, with red spots in her cheeks and her mouth pulled down.

"Why? What's he done?"

"After supper, he saw some of the things I'd drawn and he showed me some of his. His are better, quite different. He draws machines, taking each bit and . . . well, he told me what was wrong with mine but he told me horribly."

"He's always unfriendly at the beginning, you know that. He's shy . . ." She trailed away, uncertainly.

37

"It's not that, it's the way he looked at them through his glasses like an old man. And his hands were dirty and he left marks." Her face screwed up.

April tried to imagine what it felt like to be proud of something and have it ridiculed. It was almost impossible for her. She was totally uncreative. She sat too long without speaking and because her inability to help Pan made her angry she dismissed it all. It was nothing. One of Pan's moods. Mick had probably done and said almost nothing. April wanted to go back, down to the others. She began to pile the drawings neatly together.

Pan opened a drawer, her voice casual. "You might like to look at these." Her face was ordinary now. Remembering last night again, April took the big pile and Pan sat cross-legged on the floor and began to explain them.

"Our rubber, I think," Davy said, and he began to add up the score. He was pleased with the way he had played.

"Sorry about that, Mother." Paul smiled across at Susie and she rested a hand over his.

"Don't be silly, it was bad luck. You played very well." She looked down at her son's hand, big and long-fingered, and two of hers wouldn't have hidden it. "Where did April go?"

"She went out, ages ago." Paul withdrew his hand gently.

Susie pushed back her chair a little, crossing her legs. "She's changed so much, Bess. She's going to be quite lovely." Her voice held warmth, just tinged with mild surprise.

"Do you think so?" Bess was lighting another cigarette and brushing ash off her side of the table.

"Yes, I do. It's those dark blue eyes with auburn hair. Marvellous combination. And she was such a funny-looking little child. If I were twenty years younger I'd be very wary of her." She laughed, glancing to her son for reassurance.

Paul supplied it dutifully. "Stop it. You know very well how attractive you are."

Susie smiled a little. "Sweetheart! But don't you think April is pretty? After all, you are in the best position to judge."

Bess swung her head up and stared. What on earth was Susie playing at?

The question hung in silence. Paul looked down at the table, knowing he was pausing for too long and feeling the old, dreaded embarrassment fill him. Something he thought he had lost by now. "She's very pretty." He said it wrongly. Too casually. He felt warmth in his face.

A fractional pause before Susie laughed again. "Why, I do believe you've fallen for your little cousin!" Then they all laughed, even Paul, carrying the moment out of danger.

CHAPTER FOUR

SUSIE LAY FLAT in the sun, her eyes protected by twin pads of cotton-wool and her body glistening with suntan oil. "Silly to bother, really," she said, "when I'll be in Spain the day after tomorrow, but I never can resist the sun." She altered her position slightly and the heat seeped into her, slowing thought.

Bess smiled tolerantly, seeing the tightness of Susie's black swimsuit, the little rolls of flesh that squeezed out above and below. "Someone told me once, some man, that women need the sun. It gives them something essential. Men, he said, don't really need it at all." She looked back to her knitting, pulling her old sun hat further down over her forehead. She burnt so easily. She sat in the sagging deck chair, her knees spread widely and the cotton skirt holding the knitting and the wool. Her hands moved quickly and half her mind wandered. *I am a Taurus, through and through. A solid Earth type. A home-builder and a mother and I want nothing from life except my husband and my children and my home.* She dropped a stitch and smiled at herself and concentrated fully again, glancing occasionally at Susie's prone form. Gradually, the urge to talk came over her. She sorted through various ways to start it and eventually said bluntly, "How's Peter?"

Susie was quiet for so long that Bess thought she was asleep. Then she took the cotton-wool pads off her eyes and sat up, leaning on one elbow. "He's very well." Her voice lacked its usual lilt. "This holiday is a kind of last chance for us, Bess." She took a cigarette from the big beach bag.

Bess stopped knitting. "I didn't realise it was that bad."

"No worse than it's always been. It's just gone on for so long and it wears you down. His girl friends, my jealousy, reconciliation and promises, and then it all starts again."

"I'm sorry, Sus." Bess's face became hard for a moment as she thought of Peter and blamed him.

Susie saw the expression. "It's not all his fault. It never is, is it? I try and get my own back. It doesn't seem to matter as long as the boys don't know."

The rather pathetic cynicism in her sister's face stung Bess. "Stop enjoying your role or you'll never save anything. You do enjoy it, don't you? Having your revenge, as you call it?"

Susie's face faltered comically as her sympathiser turned accuser. "No. No I don't. Whatever I pretend, all I want is peace. But I should enjoy it. I watch him with those girls — promiscuous little . . ." Her mouth twisted into something old. "The cocktail parties we frequent so much, I watch him there. There are always girls, pretty, young, utterly irresponsible, and so ready to respond to the flirtations of an older man with enough money to make it comfortable. I worry about the boys, you know. Paul's eighteen and those girls are . . ."

"For God's sake!" Bess interrupted, pushing her hat back and sounding harsh, even to herself.

Susie laughed and lay back, replacing the cotton-wool pads. "Sorry, I get a bit stupid about it sometimes, I know. Like Mother. Do you remember her in her tragic moods?"

"Mmmm." There was silence between them, and understanding, and they were both drawn back into the memories that would always hurt.

April put the picnic basket down on a flat rock and sat beside it, her eyes sweeping the beach as she did a quick count of heads. The whole idea of the picnic was a little alien, a little too much trouble.

"Everybody here?" Paul dumped another basket beside her.

"Yup." She smiled. "We'll have to watch the twins on this beach. Honey has an obsession about climbing that cliff." She pointed and Paul looked at the long, slender arm and not at the cliff. It was a small beach, approachable only by sea. Paul and Mick had rowed the big, clumsy dinghy, making it move quickly through the water, and Mick had his tongue caught between his teeth as he struggled to keep up, to row as hard as Paul. They had dragged the dinghy up onto the beach and it lay like a big dead fish. The twins were still in it, playing a complicated pirate game.

"I haven't been here for ages," Paul said, sitting down beside the baskets. "I'd forgotten it." He wrapped his hands round his knees and a tiny wind moved his hair. Watching him, April wanted to put out a hand and smooth the hair back. The impulse was very new, very strange.

"This is my favourite beach. I came here a lot last year when things were bad. I came in a canoe once, when it was very rough, and they were furious." She laughed. "It's so secret here, isn't it? When I was little I wanted to spend the night here, in the cave."

Paul raised his head. "What cave?"

"You must remember the cave! Over there, behind the big pointed rock."

"You mean that little indentation?" He raised an eyebrow.

"I call it a cave. It's big enough to stand in and there's lovely white sand on the floor. It's my idea of a cave — not a big, dark, dripping cavern!"

"An April cave. Small and clean and white-sand floored!" Their laughter mixed. "Why was last year bad?"

"Me. I couldn't get on with anything or anyone. Daddy and I . . . it was just bad." She spoke lightly but her face held traces of remembered hurt. Of being "difficult." She lay back and let the sun touch her face.

"I left your mother sunbathing and mine knitting. Typical of them both, isn't it?"

"Yes. And when we get back, yours will have some knitting to show for the afternoon and mine will have a bit of burnt skin." His voice was affectionate.

"And what will we have?"

"Oh, we don't have to worry yet about achieving things," he laughed. "But we could go and explore your cave."

April sat up and swung her eyes round the beach. Pan, with paper and pencils, gazing into a rock pool. Mick with a book in the shade. The twins in the boat. "No, let's swim." She stood up, suddenly shy about the bikini she had on underneath her top clothes, but Paul seemed intent on his own undressing so she slipped off her shorts and shirt and walked carefully across the small pebbles to the sea. The sun was hot on her back. The sea, ice cold and transparent round her feet. She waded to a shallow rock and sat on it, her feet playing with the water. She didn't turn when she heard Paul wading behind her. The thought of seeing him only in bathing trunks filled her with curiosity that she was ashamed of.

Strange to be so conscious of bodies so suddenly. As suddenly as Eve, she thought. She heard him plunge into the shallow water behind her and he passed her rock, splashing her as he swam. His dark head, sleek now, moved quickly through the water and he swam straight out for a hundred yards and then stopped and turned, waving to her.

She stood up, rather self-consciously, and stepped down into the water, gasping at the sudden, wonderful coldness. She swarm towards Paul very sedately. The coldness made her breath come too fast and before she reached him she turned to swim back. He overtook her, splashing her and she splashed him back, sending showers of water high over him so that they caught the sun as they fell. And they were laughing and splashing like children all the way back to the shallows and all the reserve between them had snapped. April's hair was completely wet and it clung down across her neck and shoulders and it was dark red-brown. She dipped her head backwards, to smooth her hair, and her neck arched towards the sun.

"Marvellous." Paul spread towels on the flat rock and they lay there. He folded an arm under his head. "I like the bikini." All the tension between them came back.

"Do you?" She made her voice casual. "Yes, I quite like it too." The sun came through her eyelids in an orange glow. The twins were laughing somewhere, delighted bursts of child laughter.

"I envy you the twins," Paul said suddenly.

"You can have 'em. I adore them, but they need watching too much. Twins are always worse."

"Grandmother was a twin, wasn't she? I wish I'd known her, but they always seem to die, grandparents, before you're old enough to appreciate them." His voice was lazy. He leant up on one elbow and looked down at April and abandoned the triviality. She opened her eyes, narrowing them against the sun. A strand of her hair lay by his hand and Paul put out a finger and touched it. There were orange threads in it. He wanted to twist it round his hand, round and round until his hand came up against her cheek. But she closed her eyes and tilted her head away and Paul lay back.

They ate about four, unpacking the baskets and spreading rugs. April officiated, suddenly liking the status, and they came like chickens to be fed. Mick, skinny legs too thin for him, rubbing one eye and dusting his glasses. The twins came scrabbling and bouncing. Pan came slowly. She had been swimming and she was wrapped in a towel. April poured milk and coke and opened little parcels that contained sandwiches and biscuits and apples and there was peace as they ate. A short burst of tears from Mima because she wanted "orange drink," not milk.

"American millionaires drink milk," Paul said.

She studied him, skeptically, and then smiled and dipped her face into the mug. Paul grinned at April. "This game is called Mothers and Fathers."

"You're good at it."

"So are you."

The twins were off again when the food was gone, back to the boat.

"Do you want help?" Pan said, standing up obviously. "Or else I might just go and clear up my drawing things."

"I can do it."

"Paul," Mick said, pushing his hands into his pockets, "I've found a starfish that shouldn't be on a British beach at all." He kicked at a stone with his foot.

"Where?" Paul said, and they went across the beach together.

Left alone, April crumpled paper into baskets and folded rugs and liked the feeling. She liked the smile that had come to her face as she watched Paul go with Mick. She collected coke and milk bottles and screwed tops onto sugar and and jam jars. Pan came back, dressed again, carrying her small drawing case.

"I've finished now."

"I've done it all. There wasn't much." April felt a sudden, inexplicable pity for Pan. "Can I see what you've done?"

"If you like." Pan opened the case and handed her a sketchbook, watching April's reactions closely.

"You know these are good, Pan. Why do you let Mick annoy you? His drawings aren't alive like yours." She looked up at Pan and saw her for the first time as you suddenly see a brother or sister. Round-faced, pink from the sun, short, closely-curling hair and plump arms and knees.

47

Pan scooped the book away from her. "You don't know anything about it."

A few months ago, April would have snapped back. Now she merely shrugged, widening the gulf between them hugely.

They were all rather quiet going back. They all wore the baked-dry feeling that comes from a day in the sun. The tide was against them and the dinghy moved slowly through the water. They dragged it a little way up the slipway and straggled up to the house with baskets and none of them said anything.

It was a good evening, Pan admitted to herself. Bess had made meringues and they had eaten the crab and the adults were affectionate with one another because Susie was going tomorrow. It didn't matter how short a time someone stayed, people were always affectionate the evening before they went. Like the last evening of term. They sat round the fire and had coffee and tonight the barriers were down. Pan sat in safety, knowing that Bess wouldn't suddenly hint about bed or Susie laugh at "that child's serious face!" Pan loved Susie who, in turn, treated her with tolerant affection. "My little artist niece," and Pan would squirm with awkwardness because Mick drew so much better and Susie didn't call him "my little artist son." Pan wanted to do things for Susie and she would stand sometimes watching her aunt until Susie became irritated and said, "Run along." Pan had tried to call her "Aunt Susie." She liked the sound of it. Susie said, "I really can't stand it, Bess. It makes me feel sixty. Can't you stop her?"

"Does it matter?" Bess said, but she told Pan. "Don't call Susie 'Aunt,' Pan, she doesn't like it."

Davy was smoking a cigar and the smell of it mingled with the wood smoke and Pan knew, suddenly, what gave this room its own particular smell. Years and years of smoke, wood smoke and cigars and cigarettes, impregnated in the walls and curtains. She looked up at her grandfather. He stared down from his portrait, his face frozen forever in pomposity. He made her feel clumsy. A soft, struggling thing. So she grinned at him because he could never grin back.

This room was divided into people talking quietly, isolated by their topics. Her father talking to Mick, surprisingly kindly as though he were interested. April and Paul, their words a kind of excuse for exploration between them, April sitting with her head a little on one side, conscious of the way she looked, using her face a lot. Bess and Susie. Edging forward imperceptibly, Pan tuned in to this last group, sensing that what they said was what really mattered in the room. Their voices were low but by leaning forward and prodding the fire she could hear what they said.

"I'm almost afraid to go back, Bess." Susie wore silk trousers and her hands moved restlessly against the arm of the chair. Bess answered with a sympathetic silence and Pan quickened, listening intently now. "I keep wondering when things began to change, trying to pinpoint a definite occasion to date it all from." She looked up quickly at Paul and saw that he wasn't listening. "I suppose at best we'll stop scratching at each other but I'll be watching every little bikini-clad figure on the beach and wondering." Her face, without its usual assumed expressions, was sad.

Bess groped for words, trying to imagine Davy being unfaithful again and again. The thought was absurd. She took refuge in a platitude. "It might work out really well." Then she was quiet, her attention drawn to the room for a moment by the flickering of the fire or the light from the lamp flaming in Pan's hair or April's face. She wanted to hold her children forever, to keep them wrapped away from unhappiness. She saw, in April's face, a change. There was a woman in there somewhere. Something new about the mouth, and her eyelids, when she lowered them, hid eyes that knew more than Bess had suspected. Bess smiled. What better person for April to practise a little with than Paul?

Susie changed the subject abruptly and so much along the lines Bess had been thinking that Bess jumped. "They look nice together, the children." Her voice was odd.

"April and Paul?"

"Yes." Susie crushed her cigarette like a wasp and her voice went low and Pan couldn't hear any more. "Bess, this sounds nasty but keep an eye on them."

Bess looked blank. "Whatever for?" Then she looked hard at Susie, willing her not to say it.

"Well, April is lovely and there's something

about the way she uses her eyes and moves her body that's . . . well, Paul's eighteen and . . ." She waved her hands and made a little world-weary face.

For a second Bess hated her passionately, seeing her jealousy in all its ugliness, thinking, *Does Peter really do all she says, or does she see that too, before it's happened?* "I really don't think it's necessary."

"You're probably right." Susie's face was sad again, her voice forgot to be quiet. "Perhaps I've got an obsession." She saw she had lost Bess's sympathy and she switched tacks. "This place is lovely, Bess, but I think it makes me a little odd. Mother . . . I can't help remembering."

Silence and they were drawn back together into memories too painful to forget. Memories so linked with this place. Memories born when they had been younger and brittle. Bess and Susie's mother, Molly James, had been a beautiful woman, too tall for her generation. Everything about her was half as big again. Her eyes, her long mouth, her laughter and her tears. Nothing to stabilise her. Her first husband died. Molly married again and appeared to settle happily with her second husband. She bore him two daughters and a son. A glorious, big, laughing son. The hysteria which was crouching dormant in her never emerged until her son was killed in the second year of the second war. The sadness of losing Charles had bitten into them all deeply, but it cut something right through in Molly. Her husband had no idea how to cope with the thing his wife became. Molly had come down to stay at this house one summer. April had been three, a delightful, impish little thing and Bess, seeing how Molly loved her, had prayed for a miracle. Her second child was heavy inside her. It seemed so good. Molly was calm. She liked Davy and he was good with her, weathering her moods. And then, suddenly, the sixth day of her stay, floundering in one of her depressions, Molly went down to the beach to swim and was drowned. No one ever analysed it too closely. Bess shivered.

"I'm sorry, I'm absurd." Susie dragged them out of the past. For a moment, Bess thought her sincere, but Susie's hands were spread theatrically. Jealousy, Bess thought, was a hideous, hideous thing.

Pan heard their voices stop. She had registered the pause when both their faces had become suddenly different. Very still, frightening her. She stared at them now as they slipped into chatter and curiosity went hammering through her.

CHAPTER FIVE

WITH SUSIE'S DEPARTURE things settled down into a routine. Days were no longer individual, they formed a chain. Bess gathered her two nephews to her and established a close, very family feeling between them all. The weather was marvellous and they became used to waking into misted heat and wearing few clothes and eating inside, almost grateful for an excuse to leave the sun, which must, at all costs, be used. The twins ran about in matching cotton bikini bottoms that Bess had been bullied into buying for them by an insistent saleswoman. Now, watching them, skinny and brown and enchanting, Bess was glad she had been weak. Mick seemed to have settled down, too, and unbent a little. Coming out of the house the second afternoon after Susie left, Bess saw him squatting on the grass, a twin on each side of him. She very quietly went a little closer. He was taking his telescope to bits for them, polishing each segment and explaining in a serious voice how it worked. They watched him, fascinated and round-eyed. Bess smiled and went silently back in again, not wanting to disturb the little scene.

The one worry Bess did have was Pan. She was behaving oddly, appearing late for meals and irritating Davy. She avoided the others and went off by herself for long stretches, but she did it so defiantly that Bess began to suspect she merely wanted attention and so didn't comment. She might feel overshadowed by the older ones, or jealous of the friendship between April and Paul, but still, it worried Bess rather.

"Do you know what's wrong with Pan?" It was Mrs. Gill's afternoon off and April and Bess were washing up. They had half drawn the kitchen curtains and it was beautifully cool and April's mind had been wandering as she dried up.

"Sorry, what did you say? I was dreaming."

"Pandy. Do you know what's the matter with her?"

"Mostly Mick, I think. They just rub each other up the wrong way and they're too close in age and it's difficult for them to avoid each other here." April grinned. "Yesterday, on the beach, she threw a great bit of seaweed at him. That awful brown frilly stuff!"

"I suppose they didn't actually come to blows?"

"No. I think Mick might have retaliated but Paul was pretty quick. He stopped it. He looked very fierce and said something scathing and it all faded away." April glossed over the incident, but she had thought of it several times since yesterday. Remembering made her oddly excited. Nothing — just a quarrel that suddenly grew out of hand — but when Paul had come between Mick and Pan, so that Mick stopped in his tracks and turned away, the authority in Paul had thrilled April, even frightened her a little. She imagined him turning that expression on her. The thought brought curiosity and a desire to provoke him and see what happened. Mick had slunk off, kicking stones, and April had seen furious tears in Pan's eyes as she had run back up to the house.

Paul had shrugged his shoulders. "I suppose we were as touchy as that once."

"Worse." She liked the way he had gathered her in with him. Into being past all that. She sat down, crossing her legs under her, and Paul sat beside her. There was the strange after-anger silence that made just lying back and sunbathing again impossible. She explored the silence and the friendship between Paul and herself, and that sudden glimpse of him being so different made her want to talk about things that mattered and see the seriousness in him that ran under the surface. She felt for something to begin with. "Pan's funny. She minds so much about things." She frowned a little. "I hope she grows up pretty."

"You mean that otherwise she'll be jealous of you?" He grinned, teasing her.

"I didn't mean that at all. I didn't say it because I wanted you to tell me I was pretty."

"I know. Unlike my mother!" He took ciga-

55

rettes out of his pocket and gave April one. The smell of new smoke was delicious. "My mother needs to be reminded, constantly, that she is attractive and she has little feed lines. Like the other night, when we were playing bridge."

"What did she say?"

"Oh, something about, if she were twenty years younger, she'd be jealous of you."

April felt a small, marvellous triumph. "Did she?"

"Yup. I think she is a bit jealous. She said, did I think you were pretty. I was in the best position to judge, or something like that. And I said yes, I did, and she smiled, the way she does when she isn't really amused and said, 'Why, I do believe you've fallen for your little cousin!'" He mimicked Susie brutally. "She should have grown up by now. She embarrassed me."

"She's an adult. She can't be childish."

Paul threw back his head and laughed. "How sweet! Because you happen to be forty or fifty it doesn't mean you're mature. Some people never mature." He put out a hand and touched April's arm with a quick, very close gesture. "Do you know when you start to be old? It's when your parents, or one of them, comes to depend on you, rather than the other way round." He dropped his hand.

"Then let her down and she'd have to cope." It was extraordinary, talking about Susie like this. Susie who was an aunt and untouchable. "Anyway, she's got Peter."

Paul's laugh wasn't very pleasant. "Big deal. She

can cope perfectly well. It's just because I'm fond of her that I go on playing up to her. If the crunch ever came . . ." He looked at April hard. "Have you noticed that they have this idea that just because we've both reached a certain age we'll be desperate to explore one another? I saw it strongly in Mother and even a little in Bess. It doesn't count that all our lives we've been just friends."

April dropped her eyes. "I don't like it when you sound like that."

"I'm sorry. Let's talk about the weather!"

"Don't be stupid. I like to talk properly." She was aware of this feeling growing. A sharp-edged feeling between them.

"What do you mean, talk properly?"

"Talk about things that matter. About all of them." She looked into his face again softly. "After all, as you say, we've been friends for so long."

Their eyes touched. April dropped hers first. "Let's talk then." His voice was a little husky. "And perhaps you're right. Perhaps I should let Mother down over one thing." His mouth flicked up at the side.

Bess snapped April out of yesterday, her voice insistent. "Come on, dreamer, you've been drying the same plate for five minutes." The cool kitchen and a mounting heap on the draining board.

"I was thinking."

"Well, think and dry at the same time."

"OK." She began to put plates away, liking the

noise they made when she stacked them and the clean white shine of china, and she filed yesterday away in a secret bit of her mind to consider again, later.

Pan sat on the concrete block and watched a bee. It was in a frenzy of excitement over a big, white daisy. She sat very still, hidden by the tall globe artichoke plants which had run wild and grown to five or six feet, their great stalks weighed down by the spiky artichokes. Sometimes Bess remembered to cut them but most of the time they were left undisturbed to sprout mauve flowers. Pan had found her retreat years ago. It was behind the garage, a series of concrete blocks which were the foundations for something that never got built. A hedge in front faced the sea, bordering the drop to the beach. She came here, often, to be quiet and enjoy the ownership she felt and, today, to hate Mick. She knew she should be helping Bess but she needed this time to herself.

Yesterday on the beach! As she remembered, the humiliation made her cringe. The anger in Paul's face and the way he had treated her, as if she were one of the twins. She fingered the key to her drawing case which she kept on a chain round her neck. It was comforting, small and cool in her hand, and it helped when she thought of the unfairness of yesterday. She had decided to make things right between Mick and herself because she could sense her mother's agitation and Pan hated tension. So she had gone down to the beach, in her bathing suit, with a towel wrapped round her because she was so conscious of being fat. Why should she be fat? April had never been and the twins weren't.

Her mind drew yesterday for her. The warmth of the stone slipway under her feet. April and Paul sunbathing and Mick swimming. Throwing herself into her role, Pan had flung the towel aside and run down into the water. She swam very well and she broke into a crawl, her ungainly body becoming streamlined and graceful. She swam to the rock where Mick sat.

"Hello." She scrabbled up beside him. He said nothing. Pan put out her tongue and caught the drops of sea that ran down by her mouth. "I'll race you back."

"I'm not going back yet." He was shivering slightly, his thin arms and legs mottled with gooseflesh.

"But you're cold."

"I am not cold!" He swung his face to her, angrily.

Pan's blood rose. "Then you're afraid I'll win. You're a rotten swimmer anyway!" She put all the scorn she could into the words and stood up and dived into the sea. When she surfaced she heard the splash behind her and knew the race was on. She swam with every bit of herself, breathing slowly, and she reached the shore five or six seconds before Mick and stood up, dripping and smiling triumphantly.

"Fat, white pig!" He spat the words at her, furious at having been beaten and by Pan of all people, and she had reached for the slimy seaweed and flung it at him.

Her face crimsoned as she remembered. She shivered a little with misery. But one thing she was determined about — there would be no truce now. She hated Mick deeply and she would go on hating him. Even April was alienated, determined to be impartial. She hadn't helped at all yesterday. She had just stood there, watching Paul and looking stupid. Pan set her teeth against the fury that filled her.

She subdued it and stood up, not wanting to start trouble with Bess, and she went to the house, putting her drawing case down and going into the kitchen. "I've come to help."

"Too late," Bess said briskly. "Where did you rush off to after lunch?"

"I had something to do."

"Pity," Bess said drily. Then she smiled. "It's all right, you can help tonight."

Pan grinned and went out and April and Bess swopped smiles.

"I must be turning into one of those neurotic mothers," Bess laughed. "She's fine."

"Yes, you're lucky to have such straightforward children. We're no trouble, are we?"

"Not usually," Bess said, "and you go too. I'll finish."

She hung the drying-up cloths over the rail and surveyed the clean kitchen with a feeling of satisfaction. Bess registered happiness. Sun and the house and peace. She smiled, just to herself, and felt invulnerable.

CHAPTER SIX

MRS. GILL, SLICING runner beans expertly, mentioned the fair to Bess. She took it for her topic of the morning, to be discussed between bursts of song. "On the green," she said, "late this year. The villagers hate it. They say the village is too small but the fair always comes." Her pink cotton blouse was rolled up to the elbows and her weathered fingers moved deftly and she talked on and on, scattering facts about the fair. By eleven, Bess knew every detail. She didn't point out to Mrs. Gill that she had been here for years and had, in fact, noticed the fair before.

She called the twins in for their milk and they came on all fours, ambling like the spaniel. "Would you like to go to the fair this afternoon?"

"What's a fair?" Mima blew bubbles in her milk and put a bit of her long hair in the mug.

"Stop doing that. You know what a fair is. They have roundabouts and swings and music."

"Can Paul take us?" Honey said.

"I don't know. We'll ask him." They raced past her, spilling milk, out to the garage where Paul was washing the car. He had bathing trunks on and he was wet and shining where the sun caught him.

"Will you take us, Paul? Will you?" They bounced and more milk spilt, running and mixing with the puddles of water by the car.

"To the fair," Bess explained, a smile struggling round her mouth as she frowned at the twins. "Paul may not want to take you."

Two pairs of round eyes stared up and Paul stared down. "Have they been good?" Bess nodded. "All right."

Bess seized the mugs before the twins were off, chasing the spaniel round the lawn. "I'm sorry to have cornered you, Paul. Sure you don't mind?"

"Of course not." He pushed his dark hair back. He was brown now, wide-shouldered and thin and his feet were wet. Looking at him, at the smile that made the receiver want to smile back, Bess remembered what Susie had said. Paul was attractive, very attractive. He reached and turned off the hose and shouted across the lawn to April — a spread-eagled figure, face tilted to the sun, the bikini an accepted thing now. She was a beautiful honey colour all over. "We're taking the twins to the fair this afternoon. OK?"

She leant up on one elbow and smiled. "Fine."

Bess, watching them smiling at each other, disliked herself for remembering what Susie had said.

Pan and Mick were unenthusiastic about the idea, being in the middle. Too young to have the twins for an excuse and too old to go for the sake of it, but they agreed, reluctantly, to come. Paul drove them all in the car because the village was nearly three miles away and the twins were not very keen walkers.

The fair was assembled, as it had been for countless years before, on the village green. A small motley collection of sideshows and swingboats and one roundabout with gaping, peeling horses. It was fairly crowded, even in the afternoon, with the village children and late holidaymakers from the bigger, more popular resort round the coast.

They left the car and walked across towards the fair, all of them touched a little by the anticipation.

"I think I'll go and have a look round," Mick said, impatient to lose them.

"We'll all meet by the car in an hour," Paul said.

"OK." Mick wandered into the crowd, disappearing almost at once.

The twins were in ecstasies of excitement, struggling at the hands that held them. "Let's start on the roundabout," April suggested, and they moved towards it, the tinny music growing as they got nearer and the riders looking oddly demure and stilted as they travelled slowly round and round. Pan trailed a little behind the group, fighting down the surge of excitement which she felt and considered unworthy. Dingy little fair. Child's stuff! But once she was on a horse, gripping the corkscrewed silver bar, she forgot to be scathing and her face broke into a smile. Her hair was flattened against her head. The beautiful, fairly slow journey, round and round, up and down, and in front of her April and Paul, each holding a twin in front of them. They stayed on for two rides, getting the layout of the fair from their vantage point.

"What now?" Paul tightened his grip on Mima's small hand.

"Swing-boats?"

"OK."

They were part of the crowd now, part of the noise and the music and the people. Toffee apples and candy floss and they bowled for coconuts and won nothing. They threw hoops and won nothing either. April's hair came loose from the scarf she had tied it back with and it fell round her face. She pushed it back impatiently whenever she had a free hand. The twins were tireless, adorable, being predictable six year olds, excited by the things that should please them, and it was so easy to slip into the role of tolerant adult.

Pan, mellowed by the afternoon, bit back her remark to April — "You never used to wear stupid things round your head" — and offered to take the twins on one of the small cars that pottered sedately round a circular track. "I can manage both of them. I'll meet you back at the car in quarter of an hour." She took their hands and the three orange heads dodged through the people towards the little coloured cars.

Paul whistled. "How about that! I'm quite glad to lose them for a bit. Let's have a go at the rifle range. I want to prove my male superiority." He reached for April's hand easily and she gave hers, equally naturally. They walked, April thought, just like she imagined you would walk with a boyfriend, smiling a bit and with Paul shouldering a way sometimes. The uneven pressure on her hand when he moved forward or back. Lovely feeling, being with him. The people who saw must think . . .

"What do you want me to win for you?" He loaded the rifle and put it up to his shoulder.

"You're very confident."

"Of course." He took aim slowly, his rifle nestling in his shoulder and his whole body intent on the slim barrel of the gun. April watched, laughing when he missed and clapping when he hit and the thin, unsmiling woman who ran the stall totted up the points.

"Choose something from the bottom shelf, dear," she said, in a toothless voice.

"You choose, sweetie."

"The poodle please." Sweetie. What a beautiful, close, relaxed thing to say. She held out her hand for the black plaster poodle. It was fascinatingly awful. "Isn't he marvellous?"

"If you say so. Funny girl!" He took her hand

and they went slowly back to the car. The others were all there and Mick had his arms full of coconuts.

"All those?" April said.

"Yes." He smiled as if it were nothing and Paul raised an eyebrow.

"The best we could do is this dog here. Amazing bit of modern sculpture, full of depth, insight, and true beauty. I'd rather have had a coconut, myself, but April wanted the dog!"

They loaded themselves into the car, tumbling the coconuts in the boot. Pan's liveliness had gone and she was as quiet as the twins all the way home.

They could hear the fair that night. They were sitting outside after dinner, drinking the beautiful coffee that Bess made. Dark, thick coffee that ended any meal superbly. It was a warm, drifting evening and the music from the fair was faint and rather mystical.

"Want to come to the fair?" Davy turned suddenly to Bess.

"To the fair?" She laughed, "Are you serious?"

"Yes, I love 'em and I haven't been to one for ages."

"Well, all right. I'll get a scarf." She stood up, still laughing. "Don't tell your mother, Paul. I'd never live it down."

"I'll blackmail you," Paul smiled.

They watched the car go, its rear lights two red retreating spots, and as soon as it turned the bend in the drive, Mick and Pan slipped their separate ways, unwilling to stay so close to each other without the diversion of Bess and Davy.

Two days since we have been alone together, April thought. *Not since that afternoon on the beach.* She said, "The sea sounds like an old man breathing!" She filled her cup again from the coffee pot and took a cigarette from the packet Bess had left. "They are funny, going off to the fair."

"It's nice that they want to. I took Mother to Battersea last summer and as we were driving back we passed Father in his car with a girl." April was silent, unsure whether to show sympathy or say nothing. "One of his women," Paul said. "He likes 'em all shapes and sizes as long as they're young and haven't much brain." He spoke lightly, as though he didn't care one way or the other.

"How awful for Susie."

"Yes, it is rather. If I marry and it goes wrong, really wrong, I'll get out of it as soon as possible. Anything rather than just going on, disliking each other."

"This holiday might help."

"For a little, perhaps." The light from the kitchen window was reaching out and touching his face and it was thoughtful.

April touched his hand. "Don't be sad about them."

He lifted her hand to his mouth and kissed it lightly, making her stiffen. He dropped the hand. "Do you have lots of boyfriends? Funny how little we know about each other now."

"No, I don't."

"You will have."

She bent her head. "I haven't got any. The boys I meet are all my age and they're so awful. They want to touch you just because you're a girl, not because you're attractive or they like you. Horrible, hot hands."

"Everyone's like that at first. I was, terribly. It's the newness of girls. You want to know everything and do everything and they're so detached and sure of themselves. Either unfriendly or giggly. And it all starts so suddenly. Because of school, in my case. One minute girls are nothing, alien; and suddenly they are everything and all your friends are talking and people start boasting. . . ."

"Have you made love?" She asked too quickly and felt her face get hot.

"Yes. Why do you want to know?"

"I just do. I look at people and wonder if they have or haven't. Just curiosity. One girl at school slept with her boyfriend last holidays. It's made her a bit of a celebrity and yet we're nasty about it sometimes. How many people have you made love to?"

"Not people. Girls. Only two. The first time in France, on holiday. And then I've had a girl friend in London for the last year. She's a bit older than I am. Just the sort of girl Mother would loathe. I've been seeing her for a year and they've never met."

"Do you love her?"

"I did, I think, but not any more. A year is too long and we've got claustrophobic together. It's so funny, the law of things. You try and try to get a girl to sleep with you and it seems everything and then it gradually dies. It's all very primitive. If she does, at once, the chances are you won't want her so much as someone who doesn't. But if she doesn't you don't waste time with her."

"And if she does, eventually?"

"If you love her, I suppose it's quite different."

April straightened slightly, wanting to ask and not knowing how. Then she made the words come. "Do you think I'm attractive, like that?"

"Yes. Very. Only much more than just sexually attractive."

"Why?"

"I don't know." He laughed the tension away and picked up her hand. Their eyes moved slowly up to meet. Neither of them was smiling. Quite suddenly, April couldn't take any more. Too much, too soon. She got up quickly and carried the tray inside and Paul stared after her.

Paul lay awake in bed for a long time that night. It was hot and he had taken off the quilt and he lay on top of the bedclothes listening to Mick's steady breathing. It was odd to share a room again. He looked across at the mount that was Mick and noticed, for the first time, how completely removed people are in sleep. Vacant, like the dead. Only the steady breathing made the chain between life and death, the chain that Mick would climb up as he woke to reinhabit his body. Paul shivered slightly and reached for his cigarettes, fumbling on the sidetable until he found the packet. The match scratched and flared in the darkness and then the cigarette gave off a small red glow. Paul leant back more comfortably against the pillows and listened to the thick silence of the night. He was listening so much more now, to things and to people and to the things people didn't say rather than the things they did. His mind flicked briefly to his parents and he accepted that they had made a mess of their marriage. The acceptance was rather frightening. At what moment did one start to go wrong? Perhaps, Paul thought, he had already started.

He had no escape from living. He knew that Mick retreated into his books and drawings, his telescope and facts. Even at fourteen, Mick had his escape route planned and, Paul thought wryly, he was going to need it. There was no doubt in his mind that his parents would part sooner or later and Mick, who felt so much more than he appeared to, would be hurt. Paul hoped the break would come soon, for his mother's sake. He loved her very much, recognising all her shallows and depths, and he knew she would need someone else. Of his father Paul thought little. Their clashes had been strong and they had separated into total misunderstanding.

The cigarette grew brighter as he inhaled, and then faded, and Paul watched it and wondered about himself. Love? He had been hurt already, "A girl in France" he had said to April. He had been just seventeen, deep in exploring thoughts and reasons and she had been the same age and utterly unconcerned with any of it. She just lived. For one bright summer she had used him and he had followed blindly and then discovered sharply that his new-found attractiveness was not irresistible. But he had been hurt by his own efforts and this was somehow satisfactory. He had gone after her and been hurt. He hadn't been swept along.

He thought of April, sleeping in the room below, the corner room that she loved so much. She loved the whole place so much. She came to it, he saw, to be refreshed — to end and begin. He hoped it would never lose its sanctuary feeling for her. April asleep, her hair spread over the pillow, the gentle movement of small breasts as she breathed. He moved in his bed and caught his lower lip in his teeth. Hard to believe she was the same person he had known before. She had changed so utterly. Or had she always been like this and he hadn't been looking? He pictured her in his mind, building the tall, slender body and the small face and putting in the features one by one until she was whole. The curiosity of a quick mind that stirred in her eyes. Curiosity about life and men. "About me?" He stubbed out the cigarette, feeling for the ashtray with his fingers. He had wanted April tonight. She was his cousin and London abounded with girls but she attracted him as no girl had before. Her innocence made him want to shock her, but when he thought of her frightened or crying he felt pain. He thought about her future — the men she would meet and love and the one she would someday marry — and the thought of her belonging to someone else was terrifying. Revolting. Because

71

the April he wanted he had met for the first time on the beach, just a week ago, with her hair falling forward and a shirt knotted above a bare tummy and a red plastic bucket full of crabs. And her shyness then told him that she, too, had seen him as a complete stranger.

CHAPTER SEVEN

PAUL SLEPT LATE the next morning. He opened his eyes and saw Mick's empty bed and he yawned enormously. Bits of last night, of April, filtered into his mind and he was eager to get into the day. Out of bed, kicking the clothes off and grabbing his dressing gown and slippers and he went down to the kitchen, looking out of the hall window as he passed and hardly believing the rain. The long, fine week had driven all thoughts of bad weather away. He filled a mug with coffee from the pot on the stove. Mrs. Gill came in, silently, and went to the sink. She didn't answer when Paul said, "Mornin'. Where's everyone?" and he knew her well enough not to press it. She had her sombre days. He left the kitchen, mug in hand, depressed a little by the rain and the quietness.

He met April on the stairs, sleepily coming down in her white dressing gown. "Hello. Did you oversleep too?"

"Yes." She stood, curling her bare feet against the stair carpet and playing with her dressing gown cord. "Old age. I never used to. I'm going to get some coffee." She yawned. "The papers are probably in Mummy's room, if you want them. Where is everyone?"

"I don't know."

She laughed. "You're worse than me! I'll bring my coffee up to my room if you want company with the papers." She went past him, the ruffled hem of her dressing gown brushing his feet and he thought her young morning face more beautiful than anything he'd ever seen.

He gathered the scattered newspapers from Bess's bed and went down the passage to April's room, pushing the door open and settling himself in the rocking chair. The rain bounced against the windows. He heard April padding along the passage and she came in and pushed the door shut with her foot.

"I brought the pot up. I thought you might like some more. And what's happened to the sun, then?"

"Got bored and gone home!"

She made a miserable face and sat on the bed, lifting her feet up under her. "Can I have a paper?"

"Sure. Which one?"

"Any one." She grinned. "I only read the

fashion page and the headlines and my horoscope."

"Illiterate. What star were you born under?"

"Taurus, the bull. Like Mummy."

Paul rustled through the pages and found the horoscopes. " 'Taurus. A good day for tying up loose ends at work and at home. In romantic matters, something you have been speculating about could come to a head unexpectedly.' " He lowered the paper. "What rubbish. It could apply to anyone."

April held her cup in both hands. "Not at all. We'll compare notes at the end of the day and see if it was right. What are you?"

"Capricorn. 'Go all out today to achieve something you have been secretly wanting for a long time. Afternoon good for arranging financial matters.' See — it's rubbish!"

"It isn't," she laughed, "although I don't know where the romantic bit of mine is coming from." Something odd in Paul's expression as she watched him over the rim of her cup. Something that made her wonder what she looked like.

"Probably a letter from one of your admirers."

"I told you, I haven't got any." Her voice was suddenly sharp and she put down the cup, hard, so that a little of the coffee spilt. "Why do you go on about that?"

"I didn't know I did."

"Well, you do. Is it to make you superior or something?" The abrupt anger straightened her face.

"Look, I give up! I surrender." He threw his hands in the air. "Whatever I've said . . ."

"I'm sorry." She looked down. "I get angry in the mornings, sometimes." She uncurled her feet and got off the bed, the warm atmosphere between them totally killed.

Paul swallowed his coffee and stood up, still holding the paper and the change of things made him feel urgency. "April."

"What?"

"I only go on, as you call it, well, I only asked you last night. That is just once. Anyway, it's because . . . because I'd be jealous, I suppose." He spoke quietly and he was very still, watching her face change from slight irritation to surprise, her eyebrows lifting into arches.

"I don't understand."

He began to regret having said anything, but she had looked so beautiful sitting there and then being angry. He made himself go on. "It's just that you're too special for some stupid kid."

"That's not what you were going to say, is it?"

"No, but we're cousins and cousins are supposed to feel cousinly about each other."

"And you don't feel cousinly about me?"

Somehow she had got control of all this. "No." He watched her for a reaction, his heart beating hard. He expected embarrassment, he dreaded laughter, but she just stood, watching him. She felt the delicious taste of importance and she smiled, very slightly. She stood and made him feel a fool. She couldn't help it, even as she watched him being angry she couldn't help it.

"I've just changed my mind!" Paul said. He threw the papers down onto the bed and went out of the door, shutting it very hard.

He walked fast and the rain beat down on his head and slid off his mac. He headed up to the cliffs, his hands in his pockets and his chin tucked down and he gradually began to walk more slowly. He hated himself for his own stupidity. She was probably laughing her head off and when Bess came back they would laugh together. The thought of Bess laughing hurt him terribly. He loved her, her neglected face, her big soft body. She was always fair, always honest. He wanted his wife to grow old like that — big and soft and loving. He walked through puddles and the water made his wellingtons glisten like patent leather and he followed a small, winding path between dripping trees and grey stones. Out of the trees and on to the cliff top and the whole of the grey sea was spread below and he was unhappy. Gorse bushes, naked of their gold, brushed against him and he began to dislike himself even more. To come out here, like a child. To sulk! What the hell, anyway! So she laughed. So she wasn't what he had thought, just his silly little cousin and it couldn't matter less, could it? Then why did it hurt? The greyness and the rain were making things worse. It hurt so much. Paul turned and crossed the fields, his boots sinking slightly into the soggy grass. He came out onto the small road that led back down to the house. Because it was downhill all the way he walked like a clockwork toy, letting gravity swing his arms and legs. Tiny rivers running down beside the road. April. The sound of footsteps jerked his head up.

A figure was running up the road towards him, waving, mac flapping, feet slipping sometimes on the wet surface. A sou'wester pulled low over its face. He knew it was April. She reached him and stopped, panting.

"I thought I'd come and meet you." She tried a smile.

"How did you know where I'd be?"

"Well, you weren't coming down the cliff path so I thought you'd probably come this way." She was looking at him, her eyes moving everywhere but against his and she fidgeted a little. "Well, it's raining. Shall we go back?"

"All right." He fell into step beside her, his heart doing odd things.

A hundred years, a hundred yards, and she stopped abruptly. "Paul, I really came because I thought you might feel, about what you said, I thought you might think I'd laughed, or something." She looked nervous.

"You did, didn't you?"

"No, I didn't mean it. It was just sudden. Anyway" — she made her mouth neat — "I had to come and tell you. I can't bear people going away and thinking something wrong, not if I can tell them. Like fighting and then going to bed without making it right first." She made a small gesture with wet hands.

Paul smiled, very slowly. "Thank you for setting me straight. I'd better do the same for you." He put his hands on her shoulders and leant forward and kissed her rainy mouth. Just laying his against it for a long, little time. He drew away. "Now, if you want to laugh you've really got a reason."

Her face twisted quickly. "That's an awful thing to say."

They moved together, their foreheads touching, hands touching, and he bent his face down. Their "sorry's" collided. Stillness and then movement, laughter that ran from one to the other, back and forwards.

"It's fantastic, this, isn't it . . . ?"

"That you feel it too?"

"So funny. . . ."

"It must be a secret," Paul said. "They wouldn't like it."

She was very serious again. "What is it? Just that we like each other a lot?"

"More than that. For me, anyway."

"And for me. But I'm afraid of saying it!"

He lifted his head and laughed. "I've just had a mental picture of my mother, if she knew. Seriously, they would jump to the wrong conclusions, I think." He tucked her hand into his pocket and they started back down the road.

"They shouldn't."

"But I think they would. Mother started it, somehow." He grinned. "Anyway, it's exciting like this."

"Baby!" She tucked her hand deeper into his pocket. "Paul."

"Yes?"

"I love the rain when you're in it!"

The house was full when they got back, full of wet coats and gumboots and the twins having their hair dried in the kitchen, wriggling under towels. The spaniel left flower footprints and spread wet-dog smell and the closeness and laughter that had grown and grown all the way down the road home was pushed back.

"Hello." Bess smiled up from rubbing Mima's hair and she was pink-faced. "Isn't it awful? I took them all shopping about half-past nine and now look at them!" She laughed aloud.

Pan was shaking her short hair, like a dog.

"That went all over me," Mick said.

"You shouldn't stand there, then, should you?"

Davy stumped in, in his socks, a glass in his hand. "Best thing for getting wet is a brandy." He stepped over the spaniel. "Don't tell me you two went out voluntarily?"

"Yup! We're hardy outdoor types." Paul hung his mac on the back of the kitchen door and ruffled his wet hair.

"Madness!" Davy said. He stepped back to avoid Mrs. Gill who was sweeping wet boots up.

"It doesn't hurt anyone to get wet. It's just drying them again." Bess got up. "That's all, Mim."

"Well, I don't like it." Davy rested an arm lightly along Paul's shoulders, having to look up at him slightly. "Come and have a drink. This kitchen is woman-ridden!"

Paul laughed and followed him out, his boots leaving great wet prints on the lino. April looked after him, a small sweep of possessiveness making her want to pull off the boots and dry his hair. She hung on to the feeling. Unlike anything she had ever felt before. And none of them knew about it, this fantastic thing between Paul and herself.

Bess lit a cigarette and pushed back her hair where it was damp at the front. She stood, characteristically, hand on hip, tummy slightly stuck out. Like Pan stood. "What can we do with the brats if it's wet this afternoon?"

"Endless games of ludo!" April made a face. "Can't they rest for longer than usual?" She was speaking with half her mind still exploring Paul.

"Brute," Bess laughed.

"Well, they must be tired."

A chorus, "We're not," and Bess tilted back her head and laughed. And, still laughing, she held out the cigarettes to April as if it were the most natural thing in the world. April took one, in the same easy way.

CHAPTER EIGHT

THE AFTERNOON PRESSED down on them, bringing with it a feeling of being trapped and heavy. Bess, putting the twins to bed, retired herself, taking the lurid paperback she had bought that morning. She wanted to escape for a little. The evening loomed at her, promising bored children and cooking, and depressing her.

Davy sat in the drawing room, in the big chair, feet on the coffee table. He was aggressively cheerful, deep in his "father" role and trying to fight the bad weather and he caught at Pan's trailing hand as she passed. "What are you up to, Pandy?"

"Nothing." She fidgeted a little in his grasp.

"Well, how about drawing me something? A boat. Draw me a boat."

Pan smiled weakly. "All right."

"I tell you what," Davy warmed to the idea.

"We'll make it a competition. Mick's good at drawing too. Let's see which of you does the best!" Pan stood quietly in the radius of his arm. She looked across to Mick who had raised his eyes from the book. "Come on, where's your competitive spirit? How do you feel about it, Mick?"

"I don't mind." He wanted to go on reading but he didn't know how to say so, not to Davy in this mood. Then his eyes met Pan's and something in her face made him want to taunt her. He remembered the beach and the seaweed. "I don't expect Pan wants to."

"Yes I do." She pulled herself free of Davy's arm. "I'll get paper and stuff."

"It must be fair," Davy said, as Pan left the room. "A time limit of half an hour."

April, cross-legged on the rug, met Paul's eyes quickly. "Do you think it's a good idea, Daddy?" Her voice was quiet.

"Why ever not?" Davy's face assumed slight irritation. He hated to have cold water poured on his ideas. "What's your objection?"

"Nothing really." She felt herself reddening, her new-found composure deserting her under his tone. She got up and went towards the door, passing Pan, whose hands were full of paper and pencils. As she walked up the passage, April could hear her father's voice, organising, and then someone shut a door and the sounds were guillotined.

The empty kitchen gave a monochrome view of the bay. Blocked by rain it seemed to fade out into a haze, like the end of the world would look if it were flat, April thought. She sat on the window seat and took one of Bess's cigarettes. She turned as Paul came in and stood in front of her, resting his hands on her shoulders a little awkwardly.

"I think this competition is doomed."

"So do I." She looked up at him. Neither of them cared.

"I thought I'd go down to the boathouse and look over the fishing rods. I've been meaning to all week. Coming?"

"OK." She moved her shoulders from under his hands, wearing the very new relationship between them with a little difficulty now. It was hard to believe in the morning, to accept now what had been said then. Having brought things into the open, the only difference seemed to be this new tension between them. She took her mac and sou'wester off the hook and pulled on boots and joined Paul, similarly dressed, by the door. They went out into the rain and he swung the boathouse keys. The path down to the beach gate was slippery and the rocks on the beach were glistening and April was nervous.

Paul unlocked the big doors and swung them back and the damp, old smell of boats came out to meet them. April followed him in and he pushed the doors shut against the rain. He found the light switch and the bulb gave a feeble, yellow glow. April pulled off her sou'wester and her hair fell over her shoulders and she knew Paul was watching her. Watching every move. It

made her move jerkily. She went down the far
end and flicked her mac over one of the canoes
and she picked up a fishing rod, wanting Paul
to think she had believed his reasons for coming.
His laugh made her swing round.

"What's funny?"

"You are. What do you think I'm going to do?"

"I don't know what you're talking about!"
Where had all the sweetness gone? Where had
this awkwardness come from?

"Yes you do. You've acted out an elaborate
pretence of being fascinated by that fishing rod
ever since we came in." He laughed again, throwing his mac down beside hers.

"We've only been here half a minute and it's
not true."

"Isn't it?"

"Don't be superior." She leant the fishing rod
back against the wall and her eyes narrowed a
little. "Just because I told you . . ."

"I'm not being superior." He was still laughing, very quietly.

"You bloody are!"

He stopped then and came towards her. "I'm
sorry. And you swear all wrong, as though you
were shocking yourself."

She stood very still, knowing he was taunting
her. She was so vulnerable in this new role,
but she bit back the angry things she wanted to
say. She knew, instinctively, that there were other
methods. She lowered her chin until her hair
fell forward and almost hid her face and her
eyelashes fell, almost hiding her eyes. Paul's

expression changed. He touched her arm. "OK. Let's look at fishing rods."

She looked up, very quickly, smiling a little now. He stood against her so that their faces touched and she dropped her head until his heart was beating against her cheek. Straight again, she watched his face come down until the last second when she closed her eyes. Kissing shouldn't feel like this, should it? She was conscious of everything as though all her nerves were watching and feeling curious. Surprise at the warmth of his mouth and the feel of teeth and she subdued a slight horror that came with finding an alien tongue in her mouth. She closed her mouth slightly, wondering what it looked like from the outside. Paul took his mouth away and dropped a small kiss on her nose. He leant back against the wooden shelf.

"You don't mind?"

"No." She ran her tongue along her upper lip.

"Can you still taste me?"

"No." She folded her arms and turned away, feeling there was something vaguely indecent in talking about it. "Did you make it up about the fishing rods, just to get me here?"

"Yes."

"Why?"

"Because you're different with them. And after this morning we went back into being all family and I wasn't sure if it had really happened. I wanted you to myself for a little."

Softness for him. "You needn't have bothered

with all that about the rods." She fingered some rotting fishnet that crumbled as she touched it.

"Would you have come if I'd said, 'Come to the boathouse, April, so that I can kiss you'?" He was a little shy, feeling a bit stupid and laughing to cover it.

"Yes. I would have come." She faced him again. She had needed to withdraw for a moment. She smiled. Her new power ran through her, making her feel beautiful and brave. She stepped towards Paul, watching him be uncertain as she changed. She loved this feeling of being able to disconcert him. "Of course I would have come." She put her arms round him a little stiffly.

As soon as she stepped into the hall, April knew something had happened. She dropped Paul's hand. Trouble. The air was disturbed with it and the spaniel was lurking miserably by the door, wagging its stumpy tail. She looked quickly at Paul and with the familiarity came awkwardness between them again. The boathouse, the beautiful secrecy and laughter and words, was gone.

The kitchen door opened. Bess came out, her hands knotted together and her face set. "Where have you been?" she said sharply.

Paul recoiled slightly. "In the boathouse, looking at the fishing rods." His hand went up in the familiar gesture, pushing back his hair.

"I can't see that you needed April to help you!

We've had a drama. Surely, April, you realised what would happen?" She softened a little, ashamed of throwing her anxiety at them.

"What would happen about what?"

"Pan, of course, and that stupid competition. I could kill your . . ." She stopped and went abstractedly past them, her irritation forgotten as she concentrated on the bigger problem. She started up the stairs and then stopped as Davy appeared on the landing. He came down, his hand sliding along the smooth banisters.

"She's all right now." He looked oddly subdued.

"What's happened?" April said, coming to the foot of the stairs.

"Your sister had a slight display of temperament," Davy said, "and your mother is furious with me." His voice was biting. "You'd better go up, Bess."

Bess almost pushed past him and he looked up after her. The expression on his face made April want to hold his hand. "What happened, Daddy?"

He faced her, his face cold again. "Can't you stop saying, 'what happened?' A huge fuss about nothing. They both need a good slap!" He went down the passage, leaving April and Paul staring stupidly after him.

They got the story from Mick. He sat on the edge of his bed, one hand lovingly stroking the telescope and his face turned down and his voice gruff. "It was all silly. We started off and when time was up, Pan said she hadn't finished. She sort of shouted. He was angry. He said mine was better

anyway and she had to learn to lose and she
shouted and then she screamed it wasn't fair."
He looked up, quickly, and he was very much a
little boy. Frightened child's eyes. "She screamed
and screamed and he hit her and she stopped
and Bess ran in." He looked down again.

April was watching Paul, watching him smile
slowly down at Mick. "You're probably right.
Lot of fuss over nothing. Pan gets upset about
things. She's all right now. Why don't you go and
see her later?"

He shrugged. "I might."

They left him, still fingering the telescope, as
if it gave some sort of comfort.

The evening came and with it a slightly hysterical atmosphere that hung round them all. Davy
had plunged into a silent, biting mood and Bess
was chain-smoking. The twins picked up her
mood and began to whine and she took them to
bed earlier than usual. There was no sign of Mick.
We don't cope very well with trouble, April
thought. *We don't understand it.*

When Bess came down again she poured herself a large gin and tonic and sat wearily in the
chair by the fire.

"Is Pan all right?" April said.

"Yes. She's staying in bed tonight." Bess drew
in smoke, deeply.

Paul said, "I'm sorry about Micky."

"Oh, it wasn't Mick's fault." Davy's voice was
icy. "It was all me!"

"Please. Just let's forget it." Bess's unusual

anger, the rigidity of her face, frightened April.

Mick came in, almost slinking, and Bess looked up at him. She smiled, attempting to restore normality. He went and stood by the fireplace and fiddled with a wooden deer and his socks were odd. "Should I go and see Pan?"

"No," Bess said, a little too quickly. "Not tonight, I don't think. It will all be forgotten by tomorrow and I think that's the best thing. And don't you worry, Micky, it wasn't your fault at all." Her smile was a little off-balance.

Dinner was difficult, alternately made up of silences and attempts at cheerfulness that didn't come off, and they were all relieved when the meal was over. Mick disappeared early, leaving them in the drawing room with coffee. Davy had a cigar and the rich smell filled the room. Outside the rain was drumming its fingers on the windows. They all seemed to slump in their chairs, isolated by the gloom.

"How about a game of bridge?" Paul's voice made the others jump. It was more hearty than he had meant it to be.

"Good idea," Bess said, looking at Davy and daring him to refuse. He shrugged: "If you like."

"But I'm so bad." April stood up, taking cards from the drawer.

"Good practice for you then." Bess heard herself using a stage-mother voice and she hated it. The sort of voice she had used that afternoon to Pan, to Mick, to Davy. A mechanical voice to hide her feelings. She knew she had let the whole incident get out of proportion, but she seemed unable to cure it. She took her place at the quickly erected table and spread the cards with a sweep. They cut for partners. April with her father, Bess with Paul. Silence took the room, punctuated only by the crisp click of cards and soft smoking noises and voices bidding. It was obvious to all four of them that everyone's mind was elsewhere. Across the green-topped table glances collided with bids, and concentration spilt and was lost. The game limped on till ten and then it was agreed, though not spoken, that it was time to stop.

Bess stood, yawning theatrically, and put the guard in front of the fire. "Thank you all. That was nice. Will you put the spaniel out, Davy?"

"Yes." He followed her from the room and with their going some of the heaviness fell away.

Paul smiled gently across at April.

"I told you I was bad," she said.

"We were all bad tonight." He took out his cigarettes and she shook her head when he offered her one. "We shouldn't have played."

"I think it helped. It gave us something to pretend round." Her face looked small and cold. "Why is Pan like this? Each time Mother worries more." She looked to him for reassurance.

"Her age or something, I suppose. Of course Bess gets worried. Has it happened often, then?"

"Not terribly. More this year."

He wanted to touch her, knowing he could give more comfort with touch than with words. He put a hand over hers. "Don't worry about it."

"I wouldn't if Mummy weren't so funny. She's

so frightened of us sometimes." She let her hand lie under his, taking warmth from him. Then she stood, drawing her hand away, and gathered cards and scores and pencils. "Extraordinary day it's been." She went to the door and stood, resting her hand against the door frame, her cheek on her hand. "Such a lot has happened. I'm going to make some coffee."

Paul smiled. "I'd love some. A lot has happened, hasn't it?" He came across and put a hand against her cheek. He bent his head until his hair fell forward and touched her face. "A fantastic lot!"

Davy's voice. Sharp and clear through their silence. "Good night!"

They moved apart instantly and there was a long second before they called "Good night" back to him. Their voices were together. Almost childish fear touched April.

"I've changed my mind. I'm going to bed now." She went quickly out of the room.

Bess lay very straight in bed and dug her fingers down into the mattress. Her mind churned. She listened to Davy's deep, calm breathing and almost hated him for not being awake. "Davy. Davy."

"What?"

His voice made her unwilling to start the peace moves. It wasn't encouraging. It was irritable and thick with sleep. Bess said slowly, "I'm really worried about Pan. She shouldn't do this."

She could hear and feel him lean upwards,

push a pillow to support himself. She could picture the irritation on his face gradually changing to resignation. "Don't be absurd. It's happened before because she's highly strung or whatever the term is and this afternoon was just unfortunate. It touched her on the raw. If you take it too seriously you'll frighten her."

"I can't help it."

"Then turn your attention to April and Paul. They are more likely to need worrying about."

"What do you mean?"

"I saw them in the hall tonight and I didn't behave like that with cousin Jane when I was eighteen."

"Cousin Jane had a harelip," Bess said. They both suppressed the laughter they weren't quite ready to show. "What were they doing?"

Davy sighed. "We're getting ridiculous, you know. Seeing abnormality in everything!"

There was a silence.

"Susie wrote. I got it this morning." Davy stirred in the darkness. "How's it going?"

"She seems optimistic. She says they're both being sensible and giving it another try. Mostly for Mick's sake, I think."

"He's nearly fifteen."

"He's just fourteen and that's not very old."

"You could say it was damned young!"

She laughed. "Davy, are we lucky to get on most of the time?"

"Like this afternoon, you mean?" He laughed. "Don't go all whimsey on me, Bess. I just love you and I'm exceptionally easy to live with and tolerant despite hysterical children and a neurotic wife!"

"Conceited, self-indulgent, overweight . . ."

"Untidy, chain-smoking . . ."

Their laughter was quiet, as was their love-making, conditioned by years of sleeping children.

CHAPTER NINE

THE NIGHT TOOK with it the good and bad of the previous day and the morning brought sun and relief and cheerfulness. Slight shame, too, when the panic was remembered. Breakfast was smoothed with laughter and then brought to an abrupt halt when the spaniel carried in a dead rabbit and laid it, reverently, in the middle of the kitchen floor.

Honey saw it first. "Can I get down, please?"

"Why, darling?"

"To play with the dead thing." She pointed a finger at the rabbit and Bess drew in her breath sharply. Paul got up, removing the body. When he reappeared, Pan said, "Did you bury it?" It was the first time she had spoken and she did it fast, aware of Mick watching her, his mouth busy with cereal. She felt her mother's concentration on her, as if she were ill.

"No," Paul said, scrubbing his hands. "I threw it over the cliff into the thick brambles."

"The rats will get it," Bess said idly, wiping Mima's face.

"I wanted to play with the dead thing." Honey opened her mouth and showed the contents.

"Don't talk with your mouth full." Davy put a finger under her chin and closed her mouth and she rewarded him with a dazzling smile, lips clamped together.

"Do you throw all dead things over the cliff?" Mima said slowly.

Bess winced and made a smile. "No. We shouldn't really have thrown the rabbit but . . ."

"Not people?"

"Of course not." She heard herself, heard her newly found calm being weakened slightly and wondered at her own irritation. She began to stack plates, ignoring the fact that Davy hadn't finished. He chewed solidly on through his toast and marmalade, looking a little hurt.

They straggled out from breakfast, making instinctively for the beach to use the sun because the rain yesterday had made the sun precious. Towels and sunglasses, rubber rings and sun hats, were collected and they met Mrs. Gill, parking her bicycle against the garage wall. "Morning."

"Morning," April said, herding the twins with more concentration than was needed because Paul was beside her and they hadn't really spoken that morning.

The tide was very high, lapping round the bottom of the slipway, and it had filled the twins' best paddling pool. They made for it, scattering small sandals behind them. Paul spread a towel and took off his T-shirt and lay down, letting the sun attack his back, hearing April do the same a couple of feet from him. "Morning."

She laughed. "Good morning!"

"About last night . . ."

"Yes, I'm sorry I rushed off. It was silly. Just the last straw really."

"I was a bit worried too." They both rolled over, inwards, and smiled at each other.

"Cowards, aren't we?"

"Hideous cowards. And we waste time. In ten days Mother and Father will be here."

Her face saddened slightly. "I wish you hadn't said that. In fifteen days we go home." The old sadness, the sadness of a good time passing. The days went, however much you realised them and clung. They slotted together and formed a time to be looked back on. Quite suddenly it seemed to April that she spent morning after morning doing nothing, lying in the sun, swimming, watching the twins. She looked across at them now. They were sailing boats in their pool, calling to Pan to stop swimming and come. The things she and Paul had said yesterday had changed it all. Resentment. "Sometimes I hate having to look after the twins. I'd like to do just what I want when I want without thinking of anyone else."

"Shall we get rid of them?"

"Drown 'em?"

"Bit permanent." He appeared to think deeply and then he said, "You have the most beautiful eyelids I've ever seen."

"How many eyelids have you seen?"

"Quite a few; they come in pairs, you know." Looking at her, the way her small breasts became heavy against the bikini because she was lying on her side. The way she became aware, and made him aware, of Mick, ten yards away, fiddling with a fishing rod. She grinned.

"They're surrounding us!"

"Ignore them."

"OK. What will you do this winter?" She traced a finger along the stripe of her towel.

"Work, I suppose. I'm looking forward to university."

"You're quite clever, aren't you?"

"Not particularly. It will take me a long time to get anywhere in the firm. My father will insist I start at the bottom and take twice as long as anyone else to come up, because I'm his son. That's what people expect of managing directors' sons so he will do it!"

"You hate him, don't you?"

"Very nearly." His face was serious as he looked at her. "Lets go somewhere tonight, by ourselves."

The warmth of being "us." "By ourselves." "Why, today, have we started feeling there are too many people?"

"You know the answer to that."

"But we couldn't, Paul. They wouldn't like it."

"I mean really late, when they're all in bed."

"Why?"

"Because I want to talk to you and touch you." He touched her face, very lightly. "Only if you want to."

"Where could we go?" Excitement running all along her as he spoke. The seriousness of his eyes and the feel of his finger against her jaw, tracing the line of it, these things made her need to throw questions and have him solve them.

"Anywhere. To the cave if you like. It would be wonderful at night."

"We'd have to get a boat out." Problem after problem, loving the way he solved them.

"We could take a canoe. I could come to your balcony about twelve — Romeo and Juliet stuff! There should be a good moon tonight." He watched her, knowing she would say yes, but still loving the anticipation.

She rolled over onto her back, her arm under her head and her eyes closed against the sun. "All right." The smile stayed on her face as if it lived there.

All the afternoon, all the evening, April felt strange. She was conscious of slight guilt and then it would be followed by a shiver of anticipation. And she felt that Bess must know something because everything was so changed between Paul and herself. The super-awareness. The way he didn't look at her, she didn't look at him. The consciousness of bodies, of touching. Simple things like sitting next to each other became charged with meaning. Handing a plate, when he fetched her sweater, when she threw the big beach ball at him. When they walked side by side. Everything was utterly changed. Looking at him, again and again, and loving the way he looked. The awareness of herself, of her eyes and mouth, her body, the way she walked.

She was conscious of everything else, too, far more deeply. Of the slightly false warmth Bess was spreading to wipe out all memory of yesterday. Of Davy's obvious good humour, of Pan's slight embarrassment each time Mick came in or went out. Of Mick himself, being a little too busy. A long afternoon, a huge tea and Bess had made a fruitcake April didn't really feel like eating, which was extraordinary.

She went to bed early and then regretted it because she certainly couldn't sleep. So she found a notebook and wrote in it, endless beautiful words about Paul and the way he looked and the way she felt. Everything had boiled up in her so quickly, just yesterday and today. She let the pen run away, taking her inhibitions with it. She wrote truthfully about his body that she hardly dared look at in case he saw her looking. *There's a lovely smooth long dent between his shoulder blades. His back is beautiful, and his neck.* She wrote of him as "lover" because she liked the word. Not poetry, just a new line for every sentence and thought, because it looked nice written like that.

At eleven, she put on jeans and a clean shirt and laid a sweater over the rocking chair. She got into bed and turned off the light and lay, still and straight, watching the window by the balcony. The waiting was delicious now. Awful — if they were discovered. When at last she heard Paul she must have been asleep, because she thought she had imagined the light tapping. It came again and she sprang out of bed, her heart beating crazily. She crossed the room and opened the balcony door and he was standing there with his back to the moon.

"Do you still want to come?"

She nodded. She wanted to go more than she had wanted anything in her life. And looking at him, silhouetted, she knew it wasn't just because it was romantic or dangerous, it was because she wanted to be with Paul. She grabbed her sweater and closed the balcony door, following him down the spiral staircase. He held the boathouse keys in one hand and he swung them so that they tapped lightly against his leg.

"Ssshhh," April said and he turned and said, "What?" quite loudly, making them both double over with hidden laughter.

The beach was a different planet at night. Quiet, no light except the whiteness of the moon that made everything look like a negative. The sea was feeble. "An old man breathing?" Paul whispered. Opening the boathouse doors was a shrill sacrilege. They carried the canoe, one end each, down the slipway and rested it on the water. Paul motioned April to get in and he held the side of the canoe. She got in carefully, taking the paddle he handed her and then he was in behind her, rocking the canoe as he pushed them off, his long legs stretching down either side of her. The canoe slipped easily through the water. As they worked their way round the coast they talked, at first in whispers and then more loudly. When April put the paddle in wrong and soaked them both, they laughed aloud, unafraid now.

They carried the canoe a little way up the beach, resting it carefully away from sharp stones that would tear the canvas. Paul held out his hand to April. "Coming?"

She nodded, without looking at him, dropping her hand into his. A slight awkwardness held her and she hated herself for feeling it. It had come as they landed.

They climbed slowly towards the cave, going carefully because of their bare feet. The white sand on the cave floor shone even whiter in the moonlight and from the mouth of the cave you could see all the night bay. April paused and looked as Paul went in, bending his head a little and spreading his duffle coat over the floor. He sat on it, pleased with the way things had worked out but a little uncertain of April again. On the balcony he had felt her wanting to come. Now he wasn't sure. She came in and sat cross-legged beside him, taking the cigarette he offered.

"It's lovely, isn't it?" Now she was the elder, in control, hiding the uncertainty better than he did. "Are you glad we came?"

"Of course." He lay on his stomach so that he could see out of the cave mouth and across the bay and he motioned April to lie beside him. She wriggled onto the coat, chin resting in her folded arms. The light of their cigarettes made the inside of the cave glow a little red.

Paul pushed his uncertainty down. "Are you cold?" Taking control again.

"Not at all."

"Good." Silence until his cigarette was finished and then he threw it away. He put his hand across April's back and up under her hair, until he found the nape of her neck. She was very still, waiting to see what he would do. When she couldn't smoke it any longer, she reluctantly threw the cigarette away and dropped her face into her arms, making no move to stop or encourage Paul. He lifted her shirt and explored the secret smoothness of her back. A quiver ran through her.

"I thought we came here to talk."

"To be with each other."

"Like this?"

"Don't you like me to touch you?"

"I don't know." She turned her face and he kissed her, much harder than before and for much longer and when she broke away her mouth felt misshapen. She touched it with her fingers. Paul's eyes were glittering a little and she could hear his breathing and his hands turned her over and found her breasts and he put his face down to them. She said his name as if it were a strange, angry word.

He dropped his head against her stomach and then leant back against the cave wall, drawing her with him so that she leant against his

103

shoulder. "I'm sorry, I got angry. You sounded so prim. I'm sorry."

Tenderness for him grew in her and she didn't understand why she wasn't defending herself. Tenderness and slight shame. "I shouldn't have come."

"Don't say that! That's why I'm sorry — because I'm afraid I've made you afraid. I wanted it to be different."

Strangeness all through her body now and a need to hold him as she did one of the twins when they hurt themselves. Trying to tell him, with the pressure of her arms and the weight of her head, that she didn't care if things weren't right. It didn't matter that she had been afraid. "I don't want to go, Paul."

"Are you sure?" He smiled, his face wicked in the half-light.

"Of course. Let's talk." She meant, talking is a form of contact we can use.

He was Paul again, understanding her, gathering her very, very close as if he wanted to press their two bodies into one shape. "About anything you like for as long as you like!"

Pan had heard them go. Because she couldn't sleep she had gone down the passage to the big window that looked out over the bay and she had folded herself on to the wide windowsill. She heard, in the stillness of the house, slight movements from April's room. Tapping. The sound of a bed moving. The soft breeze of whispering. Windows being opened and closed. She hadn't bothered to analyse any of the sounds because she was watching the bay, wondering at her own wakefulness. Then she was lonely, wanting to tell her side of yesterday to somebody. The terrible unfairness. Mick's blank face. Davy's anger. The sharp pain of his hand against her cheek. Bess's concealed tears. April. April was the only person she could tell. That first evening, April had sought her out for company and the noises told her April was awake. She would go in.

Off the windowsill quickly and she padded across to April's door and quietly opened it, stepping into the darkness and whispering, "April?" No answer. She crossed to the bed, seeing a little now, and her hands found the lamp and light flowed. The empty bed, covers flung back, was horrible when she had expected to see April's sleepy, questioning face. Pan put her face against the dented pillow and all the things she wanted to tell were beating round inside her and she hated April for not being there. For being with Paul. Pan knew, instinctively, her mind analysing now the sounds she had heard earlier. She sat up and saw the notebook on the little table and picked it up and read the words, storing them, half afraid of them and half mocking. When she got up to go back to her own room, some malicious wish to get even made her leave the book open on the bed and April's door ajar.

They came up the spiral staircase hand in hand. The canoe was safely back in the boathouse and the keys dangled from Paul's little finger. At the top step he stopped and leant on the balcony rail. "I'll go in the back door and lock it and slip the keys back on the hook." He smiled at her and it was a different smile; he had never felt it on his face before.

April said nothing. She just stood close to him, a little above him on the balcony, and thought of the hours behind. Her hands were less awkward round him now. "Let's do it again. We could take food."

"Why?" he laughed, very quietly. "Does talking make you hungry?"

She looked down at him through her eyelashes. "Being awake in the night makes me hungry. And talking. And . . ." She knew no words for the beginning of love-making. Nothing really and yet fantastic. Just exploring. Touching places in another body that hadn't occurred to her before. And being touched. Registering totally new reactions. And always the fear ready to spring out. *It's wrong. Don't.* She was exhausted by the range of feelings that had been through her that day and night and she yawned. "I'm going to bed." She kissed him on the cheek, but he moved his face, catching her chin in his hand and kissing her mouth. Beautiful, tired happiness filled them both.

She watched him go down the staircase, turn and wave and blow her a kiss. Then she went in and closed the balcony door, turned, and froze. Her throat tightened and she joined her hands together for comfort and stared at the open door. So horrible, that open door. She was still for a long time. Then, because Paul and help were out of reach and her tiredness outweighed her fear, she closed the door and undressed. She lay in bed and her brain wouldn't leave the door alone. Who? And why? For how long had it been open? And whose curiosity had it aroused?

When nothing had been said by lunchtime the following day, April began to feel a little safer. No odd glances had been thrown, no remarks that could be even vaguely connected with it had been uttered. She had had no opportunity to tell Paul, but the way she avoided his eyes and his secret hand when no one was looking made him suspect something was wrong. He thought that, today, she regretted last night and he withdrew a little after the third rebuff. And no chance to find out why. The twins were everywhere, demanding attention, and Bess was very social today, spending the morning with them, talking and talking, drawing Pan and Mick in to smooth the breach even more. And where Bess was, Davy was, and he swam that morning, delighting the twins.

They had lunch outside on the veranda with a slight wind dragging at the tablecloth. The wind had an edge to it and Davy began prophesying an end to the weather. Depression was touching him. That idyllic morning, just his family and the two boys who fitted so well, so why had he had to think of the following week? The approach of Susie and Peter. Gloom. He turned his depression into something to be shared.

"It's been amazing for September. It can't last." He filled a baked potato with butter. When Susie and Peter came things would be different. He knew he would feel obliged to watch his family and himself from the outside and try and explain their idiosyncrasies because they would be strange to Peter. The twins' wild games became absurd, their morning visits to their parents' bed, ridiculous. Pan became an hysteric and April something that could arouse Susie's jealousy. Davy hated himself for caring, secretly feeling it was disloyal to his family, but he knew he would go through it all and see them with outsider's eyes. Bess couldn't understand this. The only person she viewed differently was herself. Davy churned the soft inside of the potato into the melting butter. He had six days. Forget it. "Look, I'll take the twins to Walt Disney this afternoon. It's on in the small cinema."

Bess raised an eyebrow at him. "Are you well, darling?"

"What's the matter? Can't I take my children out if I want to?"

"Of course. And they'd love it, wouldn't you?" She iced over Davy's mood and let him be fatherly, knowing that he would be bored after half an hour and two ice creams all round. Honey would probably be sick and Mima would escape and get lost.

Bess was in the kitchen, stacking, when Davy

came in and put an arm round her waist and said, "Are you coming too?"

She laughed at him. "Of course. I wouldn't miss it for the world." The sky was visibly darker and it looked like rain so Bess gathered Pan and Mick into the excursion, ignoring Mick's pained expression. He opened his mouth to say that he didn't really want to come and Bess, ready for it, said, "It won't hurt you. You're not that old." Mick shut his mouth quickly. He knew Bess in this mood. She was working on the "friends" bit between him and Pan. He scowled. This holiday was being spoilt by Pan, by the undercurrent of dislike that had made Bess swing round and take notice and so interfere with his privacy. Mick wanted to do his own things. He rarely showed his feelings but his bad temper was obvious then, in the way he walked, in his hands, buried in his pockets, in his total silence. He even rebuffed Mima when she slipped an arm through his.

"I like you. You say 'Yup.' "

Mick shrugged and drew his arm away.

Only when they were all squashed into the car did Bess realise that she had left April and Paul.

"She didn't like leaving us," April said. "She knows."

"Don't be silly. She dragged Pan and Mick with them. And what does she know? That I've kissed you? That we talk? That we like each other . . . ?"

"That we went out together last night."

"How could she know that?"

"When I went into my room last night, the door was wide open." She spoke flatly, but the eyes she lifted to Paul's face were very frightened.

He caught the fear for a moment and then killed it. "If Bess knew, do you really think nothing would have been said? We've got to be reasonable. We're only being secretive because we don't want to start complications, not because it's terrible. You've got nothing to look so guilty about. They probably wouldn't mind."

"Yes, they would. They would. Look at the fuss about Pan!"

"That's different."

"It isn't. You think it's worth it, do you?"

His voice was sharp. "Don't you?"

"I don't know. I loved last night, being with you. I like you wanting to be with me and the way you look at me, but I don't know whether it's you or just this place I love and . . ."

"Well I do know! I've had girl friends before and I thought I loved one or two, but with you it's different." He looked strange. "I couldn't bear it if we just stopped, because of them. How can we? Or can you turn it on and off?"

"No, of course not." She watched the back of his head as he turned away. She was feeling things almost too hard for her to grasp. A need to show her need to him. She sighed. "Can I have a cigarette?"

"Yup." He lit two.

"I didn't mean to sound like I sounded."

"Nor did I. I just don't like hiding it now. All this secrecy has worn a bit thin."

"All? It's only been two days."

He smiled. "I've been hiding it longer than that."

"Since when?"

"Since the very first afternoon on the beach, really, only I didn't quite believe it."

"You just looked at me and . . ." It was beautiful. Something like that with herself the cause of it. She wanted to give him something back. "With me, I'm not quite sure. Perhaps that evening, looking at you when you played bridge, I don't know. Paul, I want it to be easy. I want to be able to say just what I like to you all the time."

"No subterfuge."

She laughed. "Well, it will probably all come out and then we'll have it in the open!"

He stared at her. "God, you sound old!"

"Paul!" She touched him. She felt so young she could hardly talk, hardly walk.

He smiled a little. "We're mad. We moan and moan about not having any peace and now we've got a whole afternoon and we're wasting it. Come on!" He took her hand, pulling her forward.

"Where are we going?"

"Up on the cliffs. In the car. Anywhere!"

They walked and ran and laughed, on top of the cliffs and along the beach, ignoring the wind and the slight drizzle. Back for tea, toast with melted butter, and strawberry jam and the afternoon was all theirs. To talk, to kiss each

111

other, to roll on the floor, for Paul to pick her up and swing her round and round. *I love him.* April carried the thought close to her, as she spoke and listened, as she touched him. Love. But alongside it ran a strange sensation. A sense of gathering speed, rolling downhill it became impossible to stop and then crashing.

CHAPTER TEN

THREE DAYS, LINKED together by three nights, with the wind getting stronger and the sun cooler. The three days formed a small unit in April's mind. The night in the cave had been the first big step forward between herself and Paul, but she dated everything from the morning when she had gone out to meet him in the rain. She acted as from that point. The way she felt was a deepening of what she had felt then. She still had the super-awareness, of herself and the people round her. Her hair she wore in bunches, in one bunch, one afternoon in plaits like Mima's. Sometimes loose. It became a way of expressing her mood. And what she put on. No longer pulling on anything because down here it didn't matter. A conscious selection process to look good. White shirts that made her browner, navy ones to deepen the colour of her eyes. She watched Bess who was preparing for the arrival of Susie and Peter and had pushed behind her her worry about Pan. Pan was better, anyway, pinker and laughing more, even able to look at Mick and sometimes talk to him. He treated her warily, still unsure of her. He would be laughing, crouched with the twins who were the only ones he could really relax with, his hair falling forward and smiling the rare, very sweet smile and Pan would come across. It was like touching a bad tooth for her. "Hello." He would look up, drop the smile, and make an obvious effort to be polite, like a child at a party. Restless suddenly and wanting to escape. April realised, with surprise, that Pan had really frightened him. The incident had affected him far more deeply than Pan. She would always shout and scream and then recover. Mick was still feeling the wounds.

A bright morning, a misleading one, and by eleven the windows were rattling under the wind. April wandered into the kitchen to make some coffee. Last night she and Paul had gone to the cave again, but it hadn't been so good. Much colder and darker and the sea had been choppy and a little frightening. But it was wonderful, being alone and having no one watching. She found Bess busy with a cake and she sat and watched for a while. It was easier to talk to Bess when her hands were busy.

"It occurred to me," Bess said, "that we haven't had a chocolate cake for ages and Daddy loves them so much when he's not dieting." She held the bowl against herself, tucked into one arm, and beat the mixture.

"D'you want some coffee? I was going to make it for everyone, but I can't be bothered now."

"They can make their own. I'd love a cup." She put the bowl down, folding in the flour with a big metal spoon. The kettle began to murmur. Bess scooped cake mixture into sandwich tins and put them in the oven. She washed her hands and took a cigarette, offering April one, "Although I shouldn't really encourage you, darling!"

The second time, April thought. She said, "Black or white?"

"White, this morning." Bess settled on the window seat, smiling her thanks for the coffee and ready to sit for a while. "You look pretty in that white shirt."

April looked surprised. She never thought Bess noticed appearances. She flicked ash off her cigarette with a practised hand. "Would you like it if I got married young?"

"Depends how young. I think if you wanted to marry before you were twenty, we wouldn't be very happy. Anyone in mind?"

"Of course not. I just wondered. Suppose I had a baby. An illegitimate one."

Bess put on her jokey shocked face. "Are you intending to?"

"Seriously. Suppose I did."

"Well, we'd manage. We wouldn't disown you, if that's what you mean. I don't think your father would do the 'never darken my doorstep again' bit. But I hope you'll wait!" Bess was grinning.

"Till I'm married, you mean. Just for babies or to make love?"

"Both. It's simpler." Bess drank deeply from the coffee cup.

"You think it's wrong then?"

"Wrong in the results it can have, in the way it changes girls. The things they look for and need. . . ." Bess shrugged. "And, of course, unless you're very highly sexed it's going to take quite some time for you to get anything out of it. I think it's better to go through that whole process with the man you marry, that's all." She put out the half-finished cigarette and carried the mixing bowl to the sink.

April waited, watching. The tap stopped running and Bess wiped her hands on her apron and there was slight uneasiness all over her.

"Did you wait?" April said.

"What a question. Next you'll want to know if Davy's your father!"

"Well, you were very pretty . . ."

"Thanks!"

". . . and is he?"

It was a joke and Bess responded in kind. "Actually he is. And if you study yourself and your father you'll notice that your eyes are identical!"

April laughed. "I hope I'm not as fat as him when I'm forty-six," and then the talking mood was gone and the question she had really wanted answered, utterly lost. But it had helped. Bess would be with her, she knew, whatever mistakes she made. Bess would understand, however hurt and angry she might be. *So I won't make any,* April thought.

By two o'clock the wind was stronger and the sea was grey and white and moving a lot. Bess leant, elbows on the table, cigarette in hand. "I hope it's better than this when your parents come, Paul."

"Rather an anticlimax after Spain," Davy said a little drily.

"Rather a relief, I should think," Paul grinned.

Bess laughed. "By the way, will you all do something for me this afternoon — if you haven't already got anything fixed up."

"I think our social agenda is clear, isn't it?" Paul smiled at April and she nodded.

"Well, in that case, there's a chest in the small attic full of old papers and things and I want a book out of it. I was wondering if you could sort through it for me. It needs tidying anyway."

"What kind of book?" Pan said.

"A family tree. Nothing special — our pedigree is hardly spectacular — but I promised John Manners I'd take it back and I'll forget if I don't find it soon."

"Who's John Manners?" April swivelled her coffee cup round and round in her saucer.

"He's a solicitor. He's looked after the family for years and he's got some idea about writing a book. When Davy and I got married, we threw all the old papers out of the desk into that chest and ever since I've been dumping things there. I'm sure this book is with them. It's flat and green

117

and bound with green leather."

Pan was looking interested. She loved sorting things. "I'll help if you like. It's Daddy's family, is it?"

"Yes."

"I don't mind, either. Old papers fascinate me," April said. "How about you, Micky?"

He came out of his silence and looked a little reproachfully at April and then at Bess. "I was going to finish labelling the stones I've collected. . . ."

Bess buried a smile. "I think three of them can manage, Mick. You do your stones."

They went up half an hour later. The attic was a tiny, low-ceilinged room, directly over Pan's. A window looked out across the garden. Paul switched on the light as they went in and the three of them stood round the chest. He lifted the lid and it was crammed with books and papers and photographs.

"Funny," April said, "I've never wondered about it. I've seen it so often and I've never opened it."

"No curiosity, that's your trouble." He flicked at her hair with a finger. "I don't like your hair like that."

"Too bad." They smiled at each other and then registered Pan and stopped.

Pan dug her hand in and pulled out an old magazine. "Shall we tip everything out onto the floor?"

"Yes, that's a good idea. Then we can sort

things into piles." Paul bent down and wriggled his fingers under the edge. "It's heavy!" He straightened up, tipping the chest, and the contents spattered out onto the floor.

"Look at this old magazine," Pan said delightedly. "Look at the clothes they wore then!"

They sorted quickly at first, then more slowly as their attention was caught by various things. The three of them, on the floor, their hands black with dust. Cuttings and recipes and baby photographs. Bits of ribbon and buttons and books. Every now and then Paul would look up and smile at April, and Pan would sense their smiles and stiffen and bend her head lower over the heaps of papers. She was fascinated, her fingers turning pages, lifting and sorting. She wanted to be the one to find what they were looking for.

She picked a small, leather book, but it was red and fat. She opened it. A diary, and her first impulse was to shut it because the diaries of the dead seemed so much more sacred than those of the living. She had seen the name on the flyleaf. Just "Molly." She opened her mouth to say, "Look, Grandmother's diary," and then changed her mind, subdued her guilt, and flickered over a page. It wasn't terribly old. It was a five-year diary and it began in 1945. The writing was like Bess's only slightly more extravagant. Reluctantly, Pan dragged herself away and slipped the little book into the pocket of her jeans.

"Look at these old postcards," April was saying. "Of the village." She spread them, fawn and curled at the edges, on the boarded floor and then Paul, opening a small writing case, found the book they were looking for.

April woke with a jump. There was a light tapping on her door and she lay very still for a second. Then she knew it was Paul and she got out of bed and went quietly and opened the door. He came in as she whispered, "You shouldn't have come this way, not down the passage, they might have heard."

"They're all asleep. Do you mind me coming?"

She shook her head, registering that she was cold and then Paul closed the door and folded her against him. She could feel the warm shape of him through the dressing gown he wore. They sat on the bed.

"Cigarette?" Paul said.

"How debauched, but I will."

"There isn't an ashtray."

"Use the little jug." Their voices were uneven, whispering awkwardly.

When the cigarettes were finished there was a small silence and April was still cold. She wriggled under the quilt, trying to make the movement nonchalant. Paul pulled her back against the pillows. His shoulder was hard to lean against and after the first stiffness she relaxed against him.

Paul stretched and turned out the lamp. They were so close she could feel his heart and smell his own, different smell. His hand was curled round her shoulder.

Very still, like that, for a long time and then Paul's hands began to move.

She began to feel unreal. The darkness, the warmth, Paul, invisible beside her, just a body against hers, just a hand and breathing and a mouth. Her brain flashed an image of Bess coming in, seeing this.

"Don't!" much too loudly.

"Ssshhh. I told you I would never . . ."

"Don't, anyway."

"OK."

She turned away from him and his arms crossed round her and they lay, fitted together, one shape. She felt him tense and then he sighed and his body relaxed and snuggled against hers.

She must have slept very soon after that. She wondered for a long time afterwards how she could have slept when everything was so strange. But she had slept and when she woke she was alone. She wondered, for a moment, if he had really been there. Then she felt the dent against his bit of the pillow, the warmth where his body had been against the blanket. She rolled over and slept in the hollow.

Pan heard the footsteps go past her door. She was awake, under the blankets and with a flashlight, her face very still as she read. She heard the footsteps and then forgot almost at once because of what she was reading. The diary: fascinating and repellent and frightening. The meanderings of a middle-aged woman who was tormented by the melancholy that grew after the death of

121

her son. Strange, terrible observations. *"They think I am mad. They don't say it but I can see it in their faces. Bess looks at me sometimes as if she were afraid."* Pan flicked through the pages and the years. Sometimes months with nothing written and then the black writing would begin again. She read of April's birth. That was a bad year for Molly. Two more years and very little written. *"Them,"* Molly wrote, and *"They." "Them"* and *"They"* were terrible to her, not believing her. Pan felt her heart rolling slowly as she read. Sympathy with this woman she had never known. *"Bess is going to have another child,"* Molly wrote. *"I'm going to stay with her."* And then, *"September. Staying in Davy's house with them. Bess is very big this time with the second baby. April is a dream child."* Page after page, then, of unhappiness, of people looking at her oddly, not believing her. *"Unfair,"* Molly wrote. Pan read, one hand in her mouth, interpreting it all at its face value. Madness, Pan thought. She was mad. *"I look at April and I wonder, the smiling child and I think will she one day feel what I feel. The hopelessness. Or will Bess? Or the unborn child Bess carries?"*

Pan read to the end. The full horror of what she knew numbed her. She shivered violently and heard footsteps creep back up the passage and didn't even think about them. *Do they know? Do they know she was mad? Or am I the only one?* She began to shake. *Am I like that? Is that why I scream?* She pushed the little book away from her and it fell onto the floor with a thud that made her jump violently and shiver.

CHAPTER ELEVEN

NOW THE HOUSE was full of people — full to the brim. Susie and Peter had arrived, hooting the car horn, loaded with bottles of wine and straw hats, and they brought the weather back. It was windy but it was very warm and the dry summer feeling hung over them all again. Only in the evenings could you taste autumn in the air. Meals had become major operations, the feeding of ten hungry people was no simple undertaking, and Bess and Mrs. Gill laboured in the kitchen. Bess was grateful for April's help which was frequent. She seemed to like helping. "I think it's incredible the way you produce these meals," Susie said, hovering uselessly in the kitchen, "but you know I don't eat much!"

"Mmmm," Bess said, a little drily.

The first day was delightful, but on the second they forgot to be pleased with each other and real personalities clashed a little. Susie and Peter were nut-brown and aggressively gay, almost embarrassingly affectionate with one another. So, perhaps, it had worked after all, Bess thought. She saw, and was surprised by, Peter's attractiveness. She had forgotten. A smallish, well-built man, grey-haired and always immaculate, he was an alien breed to her and always had been. His enthusiasm tired her. He was slightly awkward with his sons, treating them alternately with bouts of affection, which they were uneasy under, and unnecessary criticism. Bess watched Paul when his father became dictatorial and she saw that Paul only fell in with what Peter wanted because to defy him, and win, would humiliate all of them.

Susie was glowing. Keyed up by the holiday and the apparent success of the reconciliation, her effervescence bounced off them all and she was doubly alert now that she wasn't looking inwards. April and Paul were uneasy in her presence, as if even a normal friendship between them would be misinterpreted. They never touched each other, even in the exchanging of a glass or a paper or a towel, and they tried to avoid each other's eyes. Susie saw this. Her active face would fall still and she would watch for a second before springing into animation again. She made a lot of April, putting unwanted arms round her and giving her small presents. Pan watched in an agony of jealousy.

"You should wear your hair up, my love," Susie would say, suddenly gathering April's hair into her small hands and lifting it up. "It looks marvellous. You're so lucky to have a long neck."

April would smile, feeling her mouth rebelling and trying hard not to shake the unwanted hands out of her hair. She found herself noticing what she wore even more to try and alleviate the cause of some of Susie's comments.

"My dear child, you should wear a little lipstick in the evenings. She's old enough, isn't she, Bess? At sixteen I was plastered in the stuff!"

April nearly said, without thinking, "Paul doesn't like it." She choked it back.

"There doesn't seem much point down here," Bess said, reading April's expression.

"You shouldn't think like that. There's always a point in looking attractive, isn't there, honey?" Susie's hand rested coquettishly on Peter's thigh.

"Of course," he said, and squeezed the hand and smiled.

April sensed, with some kind of newly born intuition, that Susie was running a kind of contest with her. But she didn't know why or what the stakes were. Just April versus Susie. Experience versus youth?

They went to the moor, in two cars, the boots full of picnic created by Mrs. Gill. Picnics were her speciality. Masses of silver foil packages, big ones of sandwiches, little round ones which were apples, biscuits, and cakes and for Susie, whom she worshipped, a special package made

125

with brown bread. Chocolate for the twins and orange cakes for Davy.

It was a long, beautiful drive and they left about ten-thirty and drove through the small lanes and big, empty roads. Davy, at the wheel of the first car, drove fast.

Mima shook her head, her plaits swinging. "I could eat an ice cream."

"Well, bad luck," Davy said amiably. "Pass me a cigarette, Bess."

Bess lit one for him and put it in his mouth. She turned and smiled into the back of the car but she got no response. Honey was asleep against April and April stared out of the window, lost in a daydream. Sometimes the things she imagined shocked her a bit when she thought about them afterwards. Now she was in a big room and there were men with guns and one of them was going to rape her. She spun out the drama, saving up the bit where Paul came in and rescued her. One of the men, huge and laughing, tore her dress. . . . She moved abruptly, waking Honey, afraid that Davy might have seen, in the driving mirror, the expressions that these daydreams brought to her face. At the opposite side of the car, Pan was slumped down in her seat, her hands pleating the T-shirt she wore.

They stopped the cars off the road and stepped out into the big wildness of the moor. Great smooth stretches of hill and heather and air that bit into lungs with its freshness. There was a stream, chuckling over smooth grey stones, its course carved deeply into the ground. April wandered across to it, leaving the others milling about a little. She sat by the stream and felt a little traitorish, irritated by the picnic, by the twins, running in a game with the spaniel and shouting, by Susie and her "I love your scarf, darling!"

Pan came and hovered, more irritating than all the rest put together. "I'll draw you."

"I don't want to sit still." She thought, *What I want is Paul and me, alone here.*

"Just for a bit?" Pan sat cross-legged and began to move the pencil and April felt herself assume a pose. A wistful pose, her hair moving in the wind a little, her face melancholy. The sounds of the others blew down to her, shouting and the voices of the adults. They were arranged along a low stone wall, drinking gin and tonic out of plastic cups. She didn't hear Paul until he was beside her, until Pan looked up.

"Don't move," he said.

"I can't, Pan's drawing me."

"That's why I said don't move. I don't expect you to get up for me, you know!"

"If I could move, I'd hit you!" She laughed and Pan flicked the pencil aside.

Paul looked at her. "Sorry, Pandy, am I in the way?"

She stood up. "It's no good anyway." She swung back towards the car.

"What have I said now?"

"She's just in that sort of mood." April leant forward and trailed her hand in the iciness of the stream. "I love this sort of stream."

"Brook."

127

"Why 'brook'?"

"Because the word fits better. It sounds small and clean and bubbly." His hand dipped into the water. "Let's go somewhere again tonight."

"I don't feel like it."

"Why not?"

"It's all of them. They're waiting to pounce."

"They don't know anything about it. You do still . . ."

"Of course," she interrupted, afraid that he might think she didn't feel it. "Of course." His hand moved a little against her face.

"We've got so little time left. I want to use every minute of it. Five more days."

"What are you two so serious about?" Susie's voice bubbled behind them, making them jump, making Paul's hand spring away.

He stood up. "Just admiring the brook." There was a trace of irritation in his voice.

Susie stood with her feet braced against the short grass. "It's lovely, isn't it?" She wore straw sandals and her toenails were pink and her bare legs very brown. "I think Bess would be glad of your help, April." The slightest hint of dryness in her voice, making April stiffen and get up and go back to the cars, and Susie watched her go, her eyes narrowed for a second. Then she tucked her arm through Paul's and tilted up her face and the bright light of the moor showed the lines that were concealed in it. "She's so pretty, isn't she, Paul?" Her voice was warm and encouraging.

"Very. And intelligent. It's funny how you

can know someone all your life and yet not know them at all."

"You've both grown up. You're different people."

"I suppose so." Paul stared down at the water, knowing she wanted him to look at her and obstinately refusing to do so.

Susie squeezed his arm again. "What is it, Paul?" As he said nothing, she went on, "Don't get too fond of her, darling."

He did look at her then and the expression on his face made her draw away a little. "What do you mean?" His mouth was tight.

"Well, April is a sweet girl and you're both very young and it's quite understandable that you might . . ."

"But why shouldn't we? Because we're cousins and cousins mustn't?"

"Don't be silly, Paul," Susie said and her voice was crisp. "You know very well what I mean!"

"That's just it, I do know and it revolts me. Why the hell shouldn't we like each other, even more than that? I won't seduce her, if that's what you're afraid of!"

Susie took her hand away. "You're very touchy, darling. One would almost think . . ."

"And you're very jealous!" He looked into his mother's eyes and the words hung between them.

Susie lifted her chin. "Don't talk to me like that, Paul. Your father . . ."

"My father wouldn't give a damn, whatever

game he's playing now!" He felt the rage rushing into his face and voice and he saw his mother shrink from it. He turned, very quickly, and went back towards the cars, his fury going inwards now, against himself and his lack of control. He wanted to smash something and he dug his heels viciously into the grass as he walked. A little way behind him, Susie walked slowly, her face strange.

Bess had got the meal organized, rugs spread, and half of them already sitting down. She called, "Come on, you two," and April was distributing paper plates and sandwiches and the twins were feeding the spaniel with crusts. Paul avoided his mother's eyes. He sat as far from her as he could, eating without tasting and glancing occasionally at April, but she wasn't looking at him. She was so obviously not looking that Bess noticed and wondered if they had quarrelled. She wiped tomato off Mima's dress and shooed the spaniel away from the cold sausages. This was Bess's kind of thing. " 'Nother sandwich, Peter? Davy?" Family and picnic. "Micky, have a bit of cake." But something was wrong. Something too brittle in Susie's talk, in Paul's silence.

Shouting, suddenly, that stopped them all in mid-air and swung their attention towards the noise. Pan, shaking Honey. "You stupid little thing!" Paul, reaching her first and sweeping Honey, screaming Honey, away. "She trod on my plate." Pan was trembling, swinging her eyes round them all, seeing the hostility.

"Not on purpose," Honey was crying, making

the most of it, huddled in Paul's arms. "Not on purpose."

Pan's eyes searched for support and found none. Her face broke up into tears. Bess was by her, holding her, furious with herself for hating Pan's outbursts. Furious with Pan.

"You're not a child. This crying is ridiculous."

Susie came across and took Honey from Paul. "Poor little darling. It's all right." She looked into Pan's pink, tear-striped face. "You're turning into a very nasty little girl, Pan."

Peter talked loudly about the advantage of a good slap at the right time. "Never understood why girls don't get it. Do her a lot of good." A heavy embarrassment descended over them all and Bess rather wanted to cry herself. She struggled to get the mood back, flinging coffee and coke as peace offerings, eyeing Pan, who was silent and scarlet-faced. Honey, adorable with tear stains on her small face and damp eyelashes.

In the middle of it all, April had made her way across to Paul and now they sat together, half-heartedly eating slices of fruitcake, safe for the moment because Susie and Davy and Peter were in a heated discussion about children.

"Why does she do that?" April said quietly.

"I don't know."

His voice made her look at him closely. "What's the matter?"

"I've just really put my foot in it. I lost my temper with Mother." The downward slopes of his face made him look vulnerable. April looked round casually and then touched his face for a second and he swung it up to her. Incredible tenderness filled her, making her need to keep her arms very close to her sides because they wanted so much to go round him. "Let's go somewhere tonight," she said, very, very quietly.

They sat on the balcony and talked quietly, wrapped in April's quilt. Paul had come up the balcony steps and knocked on the window and they had just gravitated onto the balcony, lacking energy to go anywhere. It was an odd night, fairly warm and windless and very dark. April stretched out this new feeling towards Paul. The knowledge that he could be unhappy, that she could help. She explored her powers of comfort and she thought she had made him happier. They had talked a lot. Then silence, silence for a long time, just sitting and looking out through the bars of the balcony like small animals in a cage.

She wanted to speak again, to make him laugh. "Think of them all, asleep and snoring!" She laughed quietly.

"Is that why you like this, because it makes you feel naughty?"

All her warmth crumbled. "What a filthy thing to say."

He shrugged. "Sometimes I think you're playing."

"Well I'm not." She wanted to hurt him now because her efforts to comfort him had been useless. "Are you?"

"No." He turned and kissed her, harder and

132

you're fantastic!" He bent down towards her but she swung her head away.

"They might come in!"

"Let's go out then. On the beach?"

"No, up on the cliffs." She sprang out of the chair, dodging his arm as he grabbed at her.

Pan felt the excitement growing and she tried to control it. She didn't want to think it was good, not yet. It had been a disastrous week for her, one slight after another. Susie, her adored Susie, treating April as the favourite and April scorning the attention. *April is too busy with Paul to want anything else,* Pan had thought coldly, watching her sister wriggle out of Susie's affectionate arm. How blind they were, the adults. They couldn't see anything. They didn't know anything. Not about the diary — she shivered, remembering some of the words. And Mick, repellent and reptilian and always there, watching and irritating and enraging. Pan moved angrily and pushed all thought aside.

This was what counted. This, that she was doing now, made everything else a shadow. It didn't matter that she was fat and plain and April was beautiful, that she was unhappy so much of the time and nobody cared or even seemed to notice, that Bess treated her like a child and Susie ignored her and Mick drove her mad. None of it mattered. Not with this. She concentrated again. It might go wrong. Something was growing on the slightly dirty paper and she seemed to know how to put it down and what she wanted. Her mind was going with her eyes to the view, the lines of cliff and sky and she was drawing and seeing and turning what she saw into shapes and spaces that worked. She drew the strong, dark shape of a rock and when she had done it, the space above became sky and the space below, sea. *I've drawn without making a mark!* It was fantastic. Faster now, wanting to use the discovery in case it went away. She took a clean bit of paper, controlling the excitement, and started again, knowing what was wrong and why.

They walked with their hands lightly together and Paul shortened his step a little to match April's. They were a bit out of breath from running. Running flat out up the cliff path, jumping the rocky bits, tripping and laughing and gasping in great chunks of air. It was that sort of afternoon, that sort of feeling. Here, up on top, the wind caught at their hair and whipped pink into their faces. Paul felt his ears get cold. He was swinging April's hand up and down, up and down. He registered pure happiness. She was walking beside him, her hand in his, and she was happy to be there. He could talk to her about anything, ask her anything. He could have walked forever with her. So different, feeling like this, from all the rest.

"I'm counting time," she said, "and it's horrible."

"One more evening, four more whole days."

"Imagine never having to. Being with someone

every day and every night and not worrying if people are looking."

"You could only do that if you were married."

"Yes, I suppose so. When I think how we wasted some of it, being stupid, I could cry."

He pulled her arm and they veered left towards one of the green seats that looked out at the view. A wide, flat floor of water, moving a little, running with the clouds, licking the rocks that were spilt in it. The cliff sloped away from them, at first gradually, green and gently, and then gathering speed until it plunged in a sheer drop down to the sea.

"Clever of someone to put a seat just here. It wouldn't be so good even a few feet back."

"Mmmm." Paul put his hands each side of her face, tucking her hair away. "You look super. All sparkly. And your ears are so small and flat against your head. Bess must have been very careful with you when you were a baby."

"Why?"

"Because if you lay babies down wrong, their ears get folded back and they grow up with sticking-out ones." She laughed and he said, "Why do you look so great?"

"It's the wind!"

"Not me?"

"No, I like the wind better. He doesn't stamp off down balcony steps in tempers!"

"Cruel!" He took his hands away and they moved against each other and smiled into each other.

"Funny," she said, "I didn't think it would be

like this. Girls at school, talking about boyfriends and things, didn't make it sound like this. I never really thought it would happen to me and now it has and it's all so easy."

"It was easy, wasn't it? It just unrolled by itself."

"Except for them."

"I've been wondering about that," Paul said slowly. "We've been assuming all along that they would be horrified. But why? They're bound to think we're so young it's not worth taking seriously. They'd probably say, 'How sweet,' or something equally stupid."

"Well, we are."

"What? Sweet?"

"No!" she laughed. "Young. I mean . . . I hate the idea of leaving here, not seeing you, not feeling like now but . . ."

"You don't know if you love me?"

"I've got nothing to contrast it with," she said carefully, seeing his face stiffen a little and hating herself for the honesty she had to use.

"When I think of how little this could mean to you, it terrifies me. Are you just experimenting?"

"Not that, not again! You spoil it every time." She moved away from him, down the seat. "What do you expect me to do?"

He put his hand along the bench and touched her coat. "Marry me?" His voice was quiet and his face held a reserve of laughter, in case she laughed. But his eyes were deadly serious.

April felt her face show amazement, her hand

stop in mid-air. Then she completed its movement and brought it down over Paul's and she felt like a jerky, silent film. Completely awake, knowing that everything she said and did would matter terribly. "I didn't think about that."

"Would you like it?"

"Not yet. I want to go abroad when I leave school and find out about things. See some places, get a job in London."

"Go to a million parties and meet lots of men and I'll be tucked safely away at university and won't stand a chance."

"Yes you will."

"Bear me in mind then, while you're wrecking lives."

They laughed a little and then the laughter went away. She put her hand out and touched his face, moving it along his forehead, down his cheek, along his mouth and jaw. "I'm frightened now, Paul. As if I have to start from here, really bothering, really working out what I want for me."

He pressed her face against him and her arms tightened round him automatically as the love for him roared through her. She had crossed a line, in that moment. She was brave now.

"Some people meet the people they marry very young, don't they?"

"Yes." He was hardly breathing, waiting for what she would say.

"We could say that we'd see what happened, see if we went on feeling like this and if we did . . ."

"I will. Nothing could change the way I feel about you."

"I think I will too."

The happiness made Paul pull her against him. "Let's go and tell them and watch them collapse!"

Going back down the path, laughing, playing out the dream game all the way.

". . . and your mother, Paul, think of her face!"

"What about your mother?"

"If we announce it tonight, four days of them . . ."

"Just walk in and say, 'We've got something to tell you,' and watch . . ."

Just at the gate, April said, "We were joking, weren't we, about telling them?"

"Yes. But not joking about us."

"No." Her arms were so much better now, so relaxed round him. Her mouth was ready for his. It was one, even movement, their coming together. "I love you," Paul said.

"And I don't care if they saw that!" She snuggled against him.

When Pan stopped, she knew she had achieved something. It was a unique feeling, being sure like this. She was tired and happy and she was satisfied. She wanted to show her drawing and explain and prove what she had found out against another mind. She climbed off the wall and went in search of someone.

The house seemed deserted. She walked the

length of the passage and found the drawing room empty. She turned back and went up the stairs and the bedroom doors were closed and forbidding. She hesitated outside her mother's room but she didn't go in. The drawing was in her right hand and she looked down at it and what she saw filled her with courage. Here was the weapon to even everything up. She walked slowly up the attic stairs.

Mick looked up in surprise as she opened the door. He was on the bed, a small heap of stones in front of him, a lot of labels and a pen in his hand. Pan stood in the open doorway, a little unsure now that she had actually arrived. "Look," she said at last, and went across and laid the drawing down carefully on the bed.

He glanced at it, idly, pretending not to be interested but she saw the attention in the sudden stiffness of his hands. "Not bad."

"Don't you think it's good?"

"Not bad."

"It's better than not bad!"

He looked up from the drawing to her face and his usual noncommittal expression dropped away. "If you think it's so good why show it to me? If you're so sure! I'm not interested. I'm not interested in anything you do. You shout and cry and I couldn't care less about your scribbles!" His eyes glittered behind his glasses.

Pan stared at him and she began to laugh. "You're jealous. You know it's good and you're jealous! You've been jealous all the time. . . ."

Mick's face twisted. "Of you? Of this? It might be good for you but it's pretty . . ."

"You're jealous. Jealous, jealous!"

"I am not!" A sudden hand, with bruised knuckles and dirty nails, leaping at the paper and crumpling it. The other hand came across, pressing down, and then both parting and letting the little ball of paper roll pathetically onto the bed.

Pan was frozen for a long second. Then everything burst inside her and she sprang at him.

They heard. They couldn't help it. Bedroom doors were flung open and feet running and the little attic room was full of people, shouting, and Pan's red hatred cleared enough for her to be conscious again. Her father's hands, holding her, hurting her. Bess, in a bra and trousers, hands on her face and Susie holding a towel against Mick's cheek where she had scratched and Peter hovering, shouting. And they must be made to understand.

Pan's face was as wild as her voice. "He's mad, like Grandmother was!"

Silence fell like a guillotine. Davy's hand softened. "What did you say, Pan?" When she didn't answer he turned to Bess. "Don't you see, she's got hold of some ridiculous idea about Molly and she's been doing all this for attention."

Pan broke away from him and he took a step towards her and she shrank against Bess. Bess was stiff and unmoving. And Susie, beloved Susie, was holding Mick, who cried like a little boy and the face she turned to Pan was full of disgust.

The four faces, accusing. The tears came, choking in her voice with the panic to make them see the truth. "It's not true! I read it all! You don't know anything. About the diary, or April and Paul. You don't know about them! You don't know anything!"

Davy held the two books in his hands. The diary and April's notebook. "The evidence," he said and nobody spoke.

Bess's hands started shaking again. They had been doing it, on and off, for the last half hour. " 'Lover —' did she write that?"

"Yes."

Susie was pacing. "The little . . ."

"Don't say it," Bess said, rounding on her. "Don't you say that! Your son . . . He's your son!"

They stared at each other and all the veils dropped away and dislike was on both their faces.

Peter said, "God!" He'd been saying it at regular intervals and it was followed by a knitting of his hands and a shake of the head. "God!"

"Didn't I say it? Watch them, I said, and you virtually told me I was a filthy-minded bitch for thinking it. And what happens? This."

"Never mind who said what." Davy's face was set and older. "Where are they?"

"What are they doing, you mean," Susie said, with a small, very ugly laugh.

"For God's sake, Susie," Bess said, and her mouth was wobbling against the tears. She reached for the teapot and poured another cup, spooning in sugar, gulping down the boiling

145

sweetness, lighting another cigarette.

"It just makes me sick," Susie said. She sat on the window seat, like an old woman, no arranging of the legs or hands, spreading of skirt. She slumped. "It just makes me sick."

They came slowly up from the beach and Paul looked at his watch. "Five-thirty. Toast and strawberry jam?"

"Raspberry jam!"

"Have it your own way."

"Thanks. You could have honey, of course."

"Don't like honey!"

They stopped by the back door and April pulled at Paul's arm as he reached out to open it. "What is it?"

"I don't know. I've got a horrid feeling." She shrank against him a little. "Like when we came in from the boathouse, only worse."

"Neurotic!" He kissed her cheek. "Come on." He swung the door open, pulling her in after him.

They heard Davy's voice. "That sounds like them." He came out of the kitchen and stood looking at them and he seemed swollen, frightening. "Come in here."

For a fraction of a second April's eyes met Paul's and almost instantly she began to shake.

"Don't be afraid," he said, pulling her after him behind Davy. But she was, terribly. And she could see his fear as plainly as she felt her own. Into the kitchen, the square kitchen that she loved, and she and Paul stood by the door as close to each other as they could and swung their eyes

146

round the four faces. On the table the ordinary obscenity of tea and cups, a cigarette smoking in the ashtray. And then the sounds came, as if someone had dropped a needle suddenly in the middle of the record and the four faces she knew so well were masked with fury and horror and disgust.

Peter came forward and April thought he would hit Paul and Paul took a step back, one hand coming up a little. "How could you?" Peter looked so small, so stupid, bouncing under his righteous fury, pathetic in his rage.

"What the hell has happened?" Paul's voice was loud, to be heard, but not steady.

Susie's face was twisted into something hideous. "You little slut!" She came in front of April and Paul put an arm out, between his mother and April, shouting, "What, for God's sake, is the matter?"

"Please, please." Bess stopped the shouting, stilling them and April got in, "I don't understand!"

"I'll explain." Davy's voice was terribly even.

"Pan has told us what you two . . . children . . . have been doing!" Bess caught her mouth up at one corner, her big eyes moving frantically. "She says . . ."

"Bess!" Davy shouted. "Mick and Pan have had another row. Pan found a diary, that day you were in the attic, belonging to your grandmother. She got the idea that Molly was mad and she's been playing with the idea that she is too, hence the scenes and the hysterics. A bid for attention.

147

She threw it out today. And when that didn't work, when we laughed at the idea, she dropped the bit about you two. That you've been out together at night, making love in April's room. . . ." His face twisted and he stopped.

"Is it true?" Peter was still bouncing, jerking. "Is it?"

April was crouching inside herself. *Now, Paul, tell them now. Stop all this. Tell them we've done nothing.* Swinging her eyes to him, waiting for him to manage, to control. And realising, slowly, that he was saying nothing. That he was white and he was condemning them by saying nothing and there was guilt all over him. Realising that she had to say it.

"We've done nothing! Nothing!"

Mouths. Everywhere. And eyes. "You've been out together at night?"

"You've been in April's room?" Bess was half crying.

"Yes, but we didn't do anything." April was crumpling, craving Paul to say it, to help her, to stop it. "We're going to get married, Mummy."

Davy laughed, "Oh my God. That's wonderful!" and silence and everyone drooped.

Paul dragged himself out of the frozen silence that had gagged him. "Please. Can I explain?"

"That's what we want, darling." Susie's voice was awful, light and cruel.

"It's true we went out together at night, but only to get some peace. Because you were all watching. Because you, Mother, are so filled with hate you can't look at a man and a woman without seeing utter filth. We've done nothing, absolutely nothing."

"Don't speak to your mother like that!"

"Stop me. Just stop me!"

The hell started again. ". . . God knows what you were doing!"

"April, surely . . ."

"It's not her fault, you said, it's my son's! Well look at her. . . ."

And then April and Paul screaming, in unison, "We haven't!"

April went into a chair, looking up to Bess for sanity. Bess who was always there, always caring and understanding. Because Paul, when she needed him, was a thousand light-years away, fighting his own battle and leaving her alone. They weren't fighting as a unit any more. They were two people, totally separate. So April went to Bess, trying to make a corner of peace in this hell. "I promise you."

Bess looked down at her, tears striping her big face. She said nothing.

April laughed. "You don't believe me, do you? You don't believe me? Do you? *Do you?*"

Susie buttoned her coat and fumbled in her pocket for gloves. Her face was stiff. "I think it's better if we go, don't you?"

Bess nodded. So much that was terrible had been said that there was no way to undo it and they both accepted it.

"Yes," Susie said, "it's better if we go." The uselessness of trying again made her turn quickly to the stairs. She called Paul's name. Bess was a stranger to her, a big, untidy woman, impatient for them to be gone. Impatient to start building her peace again. *Look what the children have done*, Susie thought, as if they had spilt ink.

"I'm coming," Paul shouted. He put his suitcase down on the landing and walked to April's door and knocked. She didn't answer. He went in and she was lying with her face deep in the pillows. He crossed the room and stood over her, not wanting to touch her.

"We're going. I could refuse, but it would only make things worse. I think the more time we put in front of this the better." His voice was all right now, just. He looked down at her and for the first time in years he wanted to cry. "April, don't you think that's right?"

She lifted her face out of the pillows. Her face was red and swollen. Distorted. The ugliness made him want to shrink away a little. The tenderness he had felt for the back of her head died. "I can't talk to you. I can't think. It's so terrible." Her eyes were very red, trying to hide the accusation because he had failed her.

He sat, awkwardly, on the bed. He was embarrassed. "I know. Look, I'll write."

She made a noise, half a laugh, half a sob, but she couldn't say any of it. *What happened to our beautiful dream, Paul? We were going to get married, weren't we? It was going to last and last, wasn't it? Now you'll write.* She became conscious of something in his expression and covered her face with her hands and the agony-misery was welling up again. She tried reaching for Paul, because there was no one else. "She doesn't believe that we didn't make love. I've sworn on everything and she still doesn't believe me. She says, forget it. But the way she looks at me . . ." She uncovered her face.

Paul was completely helpless. Numb. Feeling nothing but guilt. Nothing for this girl with the red eyes. It was destroyed, whatever had been. Broken. And Bess didn't believe him either and that hurt most of all. And his mother's face and the way he was going with her, like a child, and his weakness made him want to stop thinking. Tomorrow he would think about it. But he wanted to leave April something to help. He wanted to comfort her as he would comfort anyone who felt as she felt. Only the love had gone. He tried again to find it and it wasn't there. He just wanted to get away. He knew that his thoughts were plain.

He stood up. "I'll try and make Bess believe me before I go."

"Thanks." She was quiet again.

"Well, like I said, I'll write."

She nodded. He touched her face with his hand and the gesture was stiff and useless, a bit like a film, and she hated it. He saw that she hated it. She watched him go. Then she dropped her face back into the soft warmth of the pillow, the darkness that helped a little.

Keep things normal on the surface and let the undercurrents run until they dry up. Bess

151

thought out the formula in the night as she lay against Davy's body and they went down to the fundamental basis of their marriage and felt it firm. She and Davy were still a unit.

The twins were unchanged, only sensing a little of what had happened, and Pan was an ill child, recuperating. April was an alien. She carried with her a thousand separate pieces of that afternoon and each one hurt her. Susie's and Peter's faces as they sat, temporarily drawn together by the crisis, hand in hand, when April had run down from her bedroom to try and make them believe again. April remembered their black, bewildered faces. Closed faces. Perhaps, she thought, this will make their marriage work. She smiled and was terrified that she could think and smile like that. And so many other agonising particles of that day. Davy's laugh. Bess's eyes. And Paul — Paul's silence!

She could find no comfort in those last four days as she could find no one person to blame. She dealt with them all in turn, accusing and discarding. Mick — a puppet. Back at school now, where he was happy, and forgetting it all. Pan? How could she blame Pan? She had let her sob out her apologies, sitting there, saying, "It doesn't matter. Honestly it doesn't." Not Pan. Not Susie, really, for starting the suspicions. Susie had pain of her own. And Bess could be blamed only for not believing. She had caused nothing, and had just made worse what had happened. It always came back to herself and Paul, in a way she couldn't understand.

She walked through the places she loved, the cliffs and the sea and the beach. She cried in the boathouse — the only other time she cried at all. She saw Paul everywhere and with his face came that last afternoon, back again and again. She even went to the cave, digging her hands into the white sand and wanting to stay there for a long time, to just sit in the small, quiet space in the rock, with the sea moving and the seagulls calling. To try and understand. Her bewilderment was almost the worst part of it all. One moment she had had everything — the next, nothing.

The third day something happened. She broke the last afternoon away from the rest. She was able to remember incidents on their own without the ending. She knew, quite suddenly, that this was the beginning of peace. But the house was dead for her, lost to her forever. Whatever hold it had had was gone. Just a place where she had been happy and unhappy. No great struggle now to belong to the adult world. No soul-searching. She was in it, whether she liked it or not. She began to reach back to Bess and cover, superficially, the gulf. Perhaps if the top healed, the underneath might too.

"It's the last afternoon. Shall I take the twins swimming?"

"Would you, darling?"

"Yes, I'd like to." She thought, how polite we are, still.

She sat, watching them, saying good-bye to it all. She sat on the rock she had sat on with Pan,

that first evening, her arms round her knees. Mima was shouting with laughter, splashing. April looked up to the house, down to the boathouse, back to the sea and the twins. *Paul? We couldn't cope with it, could we? After all we said.* Honey, with her hair wet. *Paul.* She spread her life out, taking everything into account that had happened that summer, needing an epilogue. One month, one summer, and a set of people who were exploded. A black plaster poodle in her bedroom and a "first love" to laugh about much, much later.

"Come on out, you'll get cold." Wrapping them in towels and they were so small and wet and full of laughter. Untouched. One hand each and up the slipway, passing the locked boathouse, all the boats put away. Watching them run on ahead as she locked the beach gate.

She held onto the bars for a moment but all of her wanted to go up to the house, to pack, to leave. The sea lapped against the bottom of the slipway and the rocks where she had met Paul were a long way under the water.